The Art of the Twist

A Collection of Short Stories
with Twisted Endings.

By.

M. H. Nana

ISBN: 978-1-7389880-3-7

Contact info: authormhnana@gmail.com

The One.

The Beloved.

Mom & Pops, Azeez, Feroz

Shahida, Taqwa, Barakah, Eesa & Rumysaa

Table of Contents

BLACKOUT

The TV screen faded to black. His phone lost its signal. A power outage, he thought. Still unsure but with no desire to escape the comforts of a worn recliner, he reached forward and flipped the switch on the desk lamp. Nothing. Jake McKee forced himself up and moved towards the motel room window; surprisingly, there was no dark cloud in the sky. He made his way to the bedside table, carefully extracted the Gideons Bible, and opened it to where the previously undisturbed bookmark tassel resided.

Almost everyone else in the small town switched their phones off and back on in hopes of gaining a signal; others ran their finger over the TV remote's power button repeatedly as though it were a rosary bead.

Eighteen-year-old Jake McKee was one of the few exceptions. As minutes of silence crept towards an hour and then finally two, Jake carefully replaced the bookmark, albeit inside a new chapter. Then, with the utmost respect, he gently laid the Bible back into the drawer. Unfazed by the power failure, he moved towards the desk, which also served as his dining table, and took hold of the complimentary pen and notepad. Starlight Motels; Shannonville, USA, he said to himself. Without electricity, the irony of the motel's name made him grin. Again, unlike most others, Jake began to develop a contingency plan. He haphazardly scribbled words only legible to him. Then, he read the list aloud, "Matches, candles, granola bars, peanut butter, soap, batteries, and novels."

Jake went to the nearest store, hoping to buy things with cash before the shopkeeper's fears surpassed his greed. After fumbling through the darkened aisles to locate items on his list, Jake hurried towards the old man behind the counter, who was more than happy to take his crumpled bills.

Sitting atop a wooden stool, the shopkeeper turned over each item before ringing it on the vintage stainless steel cash register. With the final item still in his hand, the man held it toward Jake and finally broke the silence, "Looks like you're preparing for the long haul, eh, son?"

Not wanting to share much about himself, Jake shrugged and nonchalantly said, "Can never be too prepared."

"Served our country, too, son?"

Not wanting to offend the good-natured man by espousing his pacifist views, all Jake could muster was, "Uh, no, uh… I mean, not yet."

"Well, when I served, the common refrain was you could never be too prepared."

Jake respectfully nodded in agreement.

With the items now placed into an oversized paper bag, Jake hurriedly returned to the motel room's darkness.

After lighting a candle, Jake reached into the bag and randomly selected one of the three novels he had purchased. Oddly enough, he had hoped to grab the one with the odd-looking spacecraft that adorned the cover.

Instead of a science fiction book, Jake held a book that had a photo of the sun setting over the desert gracing its cover. Why'd I buy this one, he thought. Turning the book over, he recalled selecting it after reading a reviewer's short quote beside the author's photo. Jake reread the words, "<u>The Alchemist</u> is a Must Read. A Journey Exposing Man's Desires."

Although inconvenienced by the power outage, Jake somehow found comfort in reading by candlelight. About two-thirds into the book, a slip of paper was wedged inside. Using his thumb and index finger, Jake pinched the edge and removed a receipt of some kind.

Atop the rectangular unbleached paper were the words "Moe's General Store." Beneath was a list of items he had purchased earlier in the day. Noticing the back was completely blank and never one to waste, he knew it could be of some use. However, just as he was about to place it inside his notepad, Jake noticed the word soap listed a half-dozen times and candles thrice. Jake immediately emptied the contents of the bag on the table. There were only two bars of soap and one candle. The shopkeeper had swindled him. His first thoughts were to return to the store. Instead, he opened his notepad and wrote the date and an accompanying entry. Forgiveness, he thought. And with that, he let it go.

The power outage extended past a few days. Hoping Jake would later reimburse them for the additional nights, the owners of Starlight Motel permitted him to remain a guest under the guise of goodwill. The days seemed to blend as the power outage entered its second week. One evening, a quick rap of the door forced Jake to snap from his slumber. He raced to the edge of the closed drapes and snuck a quick peek outside. Relieved, Jake pinched the bridge of his nose, momentarily closed his eyes, and unlocked the door.

"Hello, Mr. McKee!" the young proprietors of the motel greeted him almost too enthusiastically.

"Good evening, Mr. and Ms. Patel."

The couple stood trying to gauge the current condition of the room. As was his practice back home, Jake outstretched his arm in front of the doorway as a sign of welcoming them inside. Mr. Patel looked at his wife, and with a subtle shake of her head, he knew better than to accept Jake's invitation. "No, thank you, Jake. We just came to see you," he said. Unfamiliar with the local customs, Jake thought it to be a peculiar practice not to accept the offer.

In an attempt to force the conversation, Ms. Patel inquired, "So, uh, how is everything with the room?"

To avoid mentioning the outdated 80's decor, the silly clown paintings, and the lack of cable and Wi-Fi, Jake sought to be a gracious guest and replied, "It's uh, great, thanks."

Accepting Jake's words at face value, their quick smiles revealed the pride with which they owned the motel.

"Well," Mr. Patel began, "we like you as a guest, but we have been too busy to collect additional charges with the power out. And with no internet access, we can only accept cash as payment for the additional days. If you'd like to pay cash, then…"

Jake interrupted Mr. Patel's long-winded request for payment. "Mr. Patel, I used cash when I checked in. I only have about a hundred dollars remaining, and I'll need that if the power remains off. I was only planning to stay for three days, but there is no place to go right now. Why don't you keep a tab, and when the power resumes, I'll pay the outstanding balance."

Not pleased with the direction of the conversation, the petite Ms. Patel gently nudged her husband, urging him to be more direct.

"Mr. McKee, it's not that we don't trust you, but we have payments to make, too," Mr.

Patel pleaded. Pleased with her husband's assertiveness, Ms. Patel nodded emphatically in agreement.

"I understand," Jake said. He reached into his pocket, took out four twenty-dollar bills, and held it in front of Ms. Patel. Attempting to feign disinterest in the payment, she initially tried to refuse but then just as quickly clenched it. Jake turned to the table behind him, reached for his bag, and removed a credit card. "Here, take this," he said.

Mr. Patel took the card and tried to minimize the tension. He stuttered, "B, B, bu, but the power is...."

"Hold onto it," Jake said, taking the notepad and pen. He quickly printed the date at the top. Then just beneath it, he printed a note authorizing the credit card company to charge him. Unsure about the amount he should offer, he looked at the Patels, and like an attorney, Jake presented his arguments "I've been here almost two weeks, but there is no power, and no one is seeking a room in this town. What do you feel would be fair?"

Not wanting to come across as petty, the young couple sought as much as possible to make a dent in their outstanding mortgage. Shaking his head from side to side and in a singsong fashion that accentuated the remnants of his Indian accent, Mr. Patel politely returned the onus, "Oh, young Jake, you are a fine guest; whatever you feel is good, we will be happy." Disappointed in her husband's approach, Ms. Patel slid her bony elbow into his ribs and glared straight ahead.

Although Jake was allowed to pay what he felt was fair, he was suddenly obligated to pay more than he'd like. He quickly calculated about six hundred, which included a discount generally given for an extended stay. Then he subtracted two hundred since there was no power. Not wanting to waste any more time and feeling empathy for them, Jake scribbled in $500 and signed it. He handed the note over to Mr. Patel. Mr. Patel glanced at the amount, but unfortunately, it was open long enough for his wife to read it.

Mr. Patel hastily folded the paper, gave a

harsh "Thank you," and hurriedly made his way toward the next guest's room. The stern look of betrayal with which Ms. Patel stared at Jake was worse than her husband's parting words. Then, she followed her husband, seeking vindication next door at Room 7-A.

Odd, he thought. The want of money; the greed. Back home, being a gracious host meant truly caring for guests, even strangers. Even the lack of trust on their part was foreign to him.

Fearing an eviction notice would soon find its way under his door, Jake planned his next move.

Little communication about the power failure found its way to Shannonville, and any news was unofficially shared in the form of rumors at the corner cafe. Under direct orders, the local police said nothing about the cause or extent of the power outage. The officers were far too busy maintaining the safety in Shannonville to sacrifice time socializing anyway.

E-mails, instant messages, and social media

were the least of anyone's concerns. Prayers, contemplation, and reprioritizing the activities that made up their daily lives became the norm. It was as if the word "me" ceased to exist in their collective consciousness.

Approaching the end of the third week without power, Jake felt well-prepared to survive the outage. However, Jake's concern for families with children led him to share with those in need.

Almost four weeks passed before buses arrived to transport people to a camp with basic amenities. Jake relented and boarded an empty school bus at the temporary bus depot, seeking to free himself from the boredom in this sleepy bedroom town.

The bus traveled along the main artery towards Patterson, the capital city. Unmoved, Jake watched the familiarity of the place he temporarily called home slowly disappear.

Only two other passengers were at the rear of the bus when it departed. Friends, it seemed; but strangers to him. Oddly, neither made eye contact or acknowledged Jake, even as he smiled and nodded in their direction. The lack of response by either of the two men was foreign to Jake. Many memories from his childhood were examples of his parents greeting locals and strangers in their small town.

Jake had expected the bus to collect more refugees as it traveled through Shannonville and into Patterson. Surprisingly, it was only a short distance before the bus slowed and signaled to make a right turn, albeit unnecessarily, with no other vehicles on the road. The decrepit wooden sign on the main road read Observatory Lane - Dead End. The bus turned west and accelerated as it traveled along the dirt road. The vast expanse of vacated farmers' fields lined both sides of the road.

Further ahead, a forest of Juniper trees provided a canopy over the dusty road they trekked upon. A faint hum sounded, grew louder, and drowned out the bus's diesel engine. It appeared as though there was a field party ahead. Near the end of the road, the bus stopped. The door swung open. Jake picked up his meager belongings and slowly made his way to the exit as he tried to look out the dust-covered windows.

Just as Jake made his way to the exit, the driver's eyes met his as they saw each other's reflection in the wide rearview mirror. Sounding like a parent trying to comfort a child, the driver said, "You made it, boy. You made it. There is a natural spring here, food, health care, showers, and washroom facilities. The Army Reserves set it up much like one of their temporary camps overseas."

Jake responded with a long blink of his eyes and a nod. He then added, "Thank you kindly, Sir."

"No. Thank you. The outage has been a great blessing. Triple the pay plus overtime gets me out of the house away from the wife and kids, too."

Jake bit his tongue. The driver's love of wealth and contempt for his family unhinged Jake. He could not and would not ever understand.

Still carrying his near-empty bag, he stepped off the bus and traveled along the well-trodden path toward the sounds of people. Ahead was a sea of humanity. Children and adults feasted on food readily available on outstretched foldable tables. Staring at the various dishes of food nearly satiated his hunger.

Jake did his utmost to avoid using the washrooms. Eventually, he could not prevent the inevitable. Two long lines stretched in opposite directions towards the forest from the row of outhouses. Only after adding himself to the shorter line's end did Jake realize the leafy trees shaded the other line. Ten minutes passed, and Jake hardly moved from where he joined the queue. Fearing he may soon soil his clothes, Jake quickly made his way to a secluded forest area. His sense of decency bartered for relief.

Feeling better, Jake moved back toward the crowds. Under the canopy of the trees and camouflaged by bushes, he found a place to rest and collect his thoughts. From afar, the city's warning sirens sounded. Under normal circumstances, the buzz of electricity along power lines goes unnoticed. Today, however, everyone reacted as though there was a swarm of bees nearby.

"Yes!" someone yelled.

"Power, we have power!"

A celebration often reserved for a sporting championship ensued. Strangers exchanged smiles, hugs, and handshakes. Then, all contact ceased, and the chanting faded into a murmur as young and old alike reached for their phones.

As they held their thumb to the power button, hearts climbed to their throats in hopes of a return to normalcy. The sense of community formed by the collective need for survival was immediately vanquished once individuals confirmed the presence of a wireless signal on their phones.

Text messages filled inboxes indicating the arrival of buses in the next couple of hours. People would soon return home.

From afar, Jake watched as a young child

sought to share the excitement about a gold-colored butterfly that rested upon her dress. Sadly, her mom was too interested in catching up on all the latest celebrity gossip to take notice.

Then, as Jake stood to leave, a white-haired man beckoned his son. Perfect, Jake thought. He would now see the best of humanity. Assuredly, the son would pocket his phone and assist his elderly father. Holding up his index finger towards his father, the young man forced his father to wait while he searched his phone for the latest scores.

With his mouth agape, Jake stood mortified. He knew he had to take action now. He had hoped and prayed things would be more like home.

Jake remained amongst the trees contemplating everything he had experienced. Leaning against the base of a vandalized tree trunk, the sadness he felt overburdened him as adults and youth continued to interact with their phones. It was as if everyone had become faceless and ceased to exist.

With the power failure, Jake had observed something he had only seen back home. It was gone. Forever. A sense of resignation overcame him. He took off his backpack and opened a zipper. He, too, reached for his phone.

It had been about five weeks since he last held it, but it felt awkward in his hand. It was as though he were holding the phone with his right hand instead of his left. Like the others, he held the power button down. The home screen showed a photo of him with his Mom, Dad, and the family dog.

Jake missed home, and he missed his mom and dad. Two months had passed since he left. Seeking solace, Jake moved further into the forest, away from the others.

Jake had left home believing he would find people of love, kindness, and compassion. Of course, with the power out, he had seen the spirit of community in his truest sense. Yet, his experiences here exposed him to a strange and different manner of behavior. He would return home and try to find the words to share his findings with his people.

He touched the icon labeled "HOME." A text box appeared. Inside, Jake typed:

"Greetings. I had fully prepared for a test, but the length and extent of the power failure, albeit brilliantly planned and executed, was still shocking. Nevertheless, my observations are complete. When the power was out, I saw the spirit of community in its truest sense. However, when you restored the power, all was lost. I shall return home. Fearing a future in which our people may adopt the ways of these self-absorbed and uncivilized people, I recommend acting immediately. We must deploy our entire fleet of spaceships and preemptively destroy the people of this place called Earth."

FREEDOM

Three jacks. Two queens. My best hand that day. Come to think of it; it was the best hand I'd ever seen. I would have easily won. The pot wasn't much. It wasn't even money. Jeff, Steve, and I played for potato chips. With that hand, I would've won what would amount to the whole bag.

While we played, I counted the chips on the table. Eighty-seven. Barbeque-flavored, too. That has always been my favorite. Mom and Dad's favorite, too.

Maybe it was my smile. Or maybe, Jeff had the *worst* hand he'd ever seen.

"Let's quit. This is boring," Jeff complained.

"No way," I said a little louder than I'd planned, "we're in the middle of a game."

Trying to persuade Steve to side with him, Jeff countered, "Let's just split the remaining chips."

Now feeling obliged to say something, Steve offered, "I guess, okay, so long as we split 'em evenly."

I made the mistake of looking at my hand again. Worse still, Jeff noticed.

"Game over!" Jeff yelled, flipping over his chair and then lifting his side of the table so the cards, chips, and drinks fell to the floor.

I stared in disbelief and screamed, "What the.."

As I was about to swear, our caregiver, Erik, entered the room. Tears streamed down my face, which I knew was flushed with anger. Then, as if everything was in slow motion, I took the five cards and carefully placed them in the center of the table. Face down. I didn't care anymore. Erik looked right at me and nodded—the dreaded sign.

Tonight, my bed would remain empty. I was the "lucky" one.

I was only eight when a drunk driver sent Mom and Dad to heaven. I somehow survived. In a three-month coma and unable to walk, I arrived at Nature Hills Learning Centre. Two years later, I'm still here. It is my school, my home, and my family.

Erik, our nurse, teacher, and parent, is our sole caretaker. Secluded and isolated, we're expected to become better people. But orphaned and excluded is how I view it.

I liked it here when I first arrived and even more when I learned to walk again. That was when Jorgen was our caregiver; it was the next best thing to being home with Mom and Dad.

Then my ninth birthday arrived, and

things changed. Jorgen changed, and I despised the place. It remained that way for eight months.

Then, before I became ten, Erik arrived to replace Jorgen.

The day after Erik arrived, barely able to say words, I told him about the "games" Jorgen forced us to play. Erik appeared sympathetic, and some things improved. But the worst things remained, and some things worsened.

Often at night, when I slept in my bed, I dreamt about Dad. Tall and muscular, Dad would surprise Erik. Revenge. Then Dad would take my hand. It was then I would awaken to find Erik holding my hand.

My perfect hand. Like all the others with Erik, that night ended with me waking up in tears.

Jeff, the cards, the nod; it had to end.

I grabbed my underwear, jeans, and shirt.

I threw on my socks and casually approached the breakfast table. Again, it was my turn to set the table. Now facing up, the three jacks and two queens stared back at me. Angered, I set the table without touching the cards. I knew I had to get away from this place.

I looked at the door, and I knew I could make a run for it. I started for my jacket. Just then, Erik opened the washroom door.

"Timmy, table set?" Erik commanded more than he had asked.

"Yeah," I replied in a near-whisper.

"Go out and collect some wood."

Figuring this to be as good a chance as any, I protested, as usual, to avoid arousing any suspicions, "But it's Jeff's turn."

"Yeah, so? Look at the mess you caused." He added, "Clean up the cards and chips," and then, for good measure, "without the vacuum."

Protesting again would end poorly for

me. A kick or punch from Erik would make it difficult for me to run.

"Fine," I said, turning quickly to show my displeasure. I roughly snatched my jacket off the hook and stomped my feet into my boots. To leave a lasting impression, I slammed the door and welcomed the outdoors.

I ran. I ran faster into the dense woods away from my "home." I knew Erik would become suspicious after ten minutes, so I had to make the distance between us grow.

After running for ten minutes, my pace slowed to a walk. Finally, I was forced to rest. With my heart pounding in my ears and breathing loud, I tried to catch my breath while attempting to mask all sounds.

Twenty-four kilometers. I recall the Centre was about that far from the nearest hamlet. I stayed away from the service road and the forest's beaten paths.

Looking around, trees and greenery filled my view below, above, and ahead. I still hadn't heard or seen anything unusual. Knowing it would be difficult for Erik to find me, I stopped again.

Hungry. My stomach growled. After breakfast would have been the ideal time to leave, but not having to see Erik any longer helped relieve any discomfort I may have felt.

With the canopy overhead, I only hoped to hear a rescue helicopter. Not surprisingly, only the sound of birds filled the air.

Footsteps. Sounds of twigs snapping and dried leaves shredding suddenly became more defined. Hiding behind the exposed base of an uprooted tree, I waited. Silence. I picked myself up and continued west towards the sun.

Two things helped me focus. Escape and revenge. Without escaping, I couldn't get revenge. And without revenge, there was little reason to escape.

Now, as the sunset, I wondered if I'd ever see anyone again. Something about the loneliness felt worse than "home." With thoughts as my sole companion, I began to have conversations in my mind.

I pressed on. With my eyes heavy and stomach empty, I searched for the perfect place to rest for the night. A clear spot of exposed soil was where I stopped.

I dragged some branches and stacked them so they stood against the westerly wind. Not knowing enough about edible plants, berries would have to suffice.

With little wind, the mid-fall night was warmer than I had imagined. Lying against the fallen tree and with the hood of my jacket as my pillow, I tried to make myself comfortable.

After turning left and then right again, my eyes closed. Without any hands violating me, I slept better under the night sky.

The sound of a hawk or eagle forced me

to welcome the morning.

Feeling refreshed yet hungry, I again turned to the same plants for food. Then I trekked with the sun now against my back.

Enjoying something as simple as sleep without Erik made me want to be free of him forever. Suddenly, I felt more energized to climb the hills littered with nature's debris. I made the long climb and looked ahead to the descent.

Making my way down, thoughts of freedom flooded my mind. Images of playing with friends, going to school, and sleeping in my room reappeared. I ran faster than ever before until I reached the bottom.

My adrenalin fueled my movements. The idea of seeking revenge grew stronger, and I forced one foot ahead of the other.

As the sun climbed higher, the seemingly endless trek to freedom forced me to contemplate my death. Questions came to mind.

What if I fall dead here?

Who would find me?

Would they find me?

A pack of wolves devouring my lifeless body repeatedly played in my mind. I stopped running. As the trees desperately tried to shadow the unyielding afternoon sun, I sat, trying to clear my mind.

Without giving it much thought, sleep began to overtake me. As I looked west, only the sun's soft glow remained as darkness blanketed the canopy. I stood.

Wolves. A single thought now occupied my mind. I think only of wolves. I stomp my boots loudly on the forest floor, hoping to turn any away. I start climbing a large incline. Looking up, the glow of artificial light pierced the darkness. Using all the energy I could muster, I neared the summit—hopes of freedom. I ran. At the top, I looked down at the village below. Smiling. I stood and took it all in. Escape, freedom, and plans for revenge were within reach.

Hungrier than ever, I carefully descended the final hill. Nearing the end of my journey, finally, my feet touched the gravel at the edge of a dark road. I turned and took one last look behind me. I turned again. Before me, freedom.

With my freedom, empathy for my captors slowly replaced the feelings of anger. Though it would take time, the idea of forgiving Erik and Jorgen was planted. Tears flowed.

Wiping my face with the sleeve of my jacket, I walked towards the center of the village. As I walked, I felt as though something was missing.

I stopped at a restaurant and found a half-eaten meal in a foam container, and I took it outside and ate.

Feeling better, I moved along the sidewalk of the main street. This place was familiar, as though I had been here before. As

I looked at the stores and buildings, I felt the comfort one feels as you near home.

I scanned the streets in search of someone who could help. At the corner of an intersection, I came to a sudden stop. Dell's Ice Cream Shoppe stood kitty-corner to me, where Mom took me every Sunday after soccer practice.

Home. I realized this was my home and where my mom, childhood, and innocence were stolen.

I quickened my pace and looked at the street names. It has to be the next street, I thought. Above me, in full view, I read TRAYBORN AVENUE, all in capital letters. Number 14 Trayborn Avenue, I quickly recalled.

Looking down the tree-lined street, memories of learning to ride a bike with Mom and the small playground ahead came flooding back to me. My eyes filled with tears, and I missed her.

Walking along the odd-numbered houses, I look further up across the street, hoping to see the red-brick home with the dark green trim. A shiny red Ferrari parked on the driveway forced me to look there first.

There it was—number 14. Unsure as to what prompted me, I rushed across the street and, without hesitation, rang the doorbell. The door opened, and there stood Dad.

"Timmy?" he asked with a trace of doubt.

"Dad?"

"Oh my God, Timmy!"

Dad quickly took me by the hand and guided me in. Everything inside had changed. All kinds of emotions came over me, and I was at a loss for words.

"What happened? Where'd you come from? I don't understand," Dad had as many questions as me.

"I, uh, I was at the Nature Hills Learning Centre, but I thought they said you, uh, uh, were gone when Mom," I said, trying to avoid the words 'dead' or 'killed.'

"No, no, I was hospitalized and lost my memory, and I had no recollection of anyone or anything. Only in the last year I started to recall things. Just last month, I started to remember everything."

"But why didn't you bring me back home?" I questioned.

"I don't know, Timmy, but you're here now," he answered, asking his questions, "How'd you get here? What happened to your clothes?"

"Uh…" I tried to answer, but tears betrayed me again. I began to sob.

"What is it, Timmy?"

I wanted his embrace, and I needed to feel wanted. More than anything, I needed Mom.

"Uh, uh, I ran away from the Centre, uh,

… I, I, they made me do bad.. bad, uh," again I stopped. I tried to continue.

A lump formed in my throat, and the tears spoke for me.

I started again, "Dad, they touched me and…"

Before I could finish, Dad stood up and walked down the hallway. Returning with a rifle, Dad took my hand and led us to the car.

Afraid and unsure of what to say, I said nothing. Dad's anger reignited my desire to do something. For me, though, it was revenge more than justice.

Dad sped through the village streets and onto the service road. We covered the distance I trekked in only a short time, and Dad's demeanor changed very little, and he said even less.

We turned left into the entrance of Nature Hills. With such speed, Dad's driving on the dirt driveway created a storm of dust behind us.

Still enraged, Dad left the car running as he climbed out and slammed the door. Dad motioned for me to get out from in front of the vehicle. Our loud arrival prevented us from surprising Erik.

Seconds later, Erik stepped out the front door I had slammed days earlier. Erik's large and muscular silhouette filled the doorway.

My concern was not for me but for Dad.

Dad returned to the car.

The gun, I thought. My hopes for freedom resting with a bullet

I looked right at Erik, knowing everything would be better. I heard the car door open and shut. Still staring at Erik, I waited for Dad to return to my side with the gun.

Hearing tires rolling on the gravel, I turned to see Dad driving away.

SOLD

Another tear rolled down my face. I sat on the top step of the stairs to the basement and just looked down. Why do we have to move? I repeated. Memories flooded my mind.

Mom came down these steps with twenty brightly-colored balloons on my fifth birthday.

And the time Mom and I tried to paint a chair and spilled paint everywhere.

Or when we both dressed up as pirates and pranced around the basement like it was a real ship

Why do we have to move? I love this place. This is home. There was nothing left to see. Everything packed. Now even my voice echoed.

"This is home!" I yelled.

"Is home… is home," the room repeated.

I heard the moving van backing up the driveway.

"Jeremy," called my stepmom, Lori.

She opened the door and helped me up.

"It'll be okay, I promise," she encouraged.

I stood up and started to leave. She stood looking down into the basement. No memories for her. I pushed.

The movers would find Lori's lifeless body at the bottom of the stairs, just like Mom.

Gift of Love

Here ya go, sir. Both phones have cases and are secured with the latest apps. Click the power button, and you're good to go. Would you like them wrapped?"

"Well, yeah," the burly customer in the police uniform responded, "I spent almost two grand. Maybe, free delivery should be included." He alone laughed at his joke. Sergeant Carson patiently watched as the young sales rep painstakingly wrapped the two beautifully logo-embossed boxes for the twins' birthday.

With the phones in hand, he exited the store. He longed for the days when building blocks were the perfect gift. At age 14, their gifts cost more than a mortgage payment.

The kids, as he still called them, had yet to arrive from school. He took the gifts and placed them inside his gun cabinet. He carefully relocked the cabinet and, as always, checked it twice more.

Sergeant Carson planned to return to the station to collect things when his wife, Karla, unexpectedly arrived home early. He hastily made his way outside and halfway down the steps. As she carried the grocery bags, she playfully nudged him and added, "Nice socks."

"Everything okay?" he asked.

"Yeah, Bob was in a great mood and let us leave early."

"Just when you think you have Bob figured out, he does something nice."

They both chuckled as they put things away.

"I was gonna head back to the station," he said, "but I'll just stay now."

"Did ya remember the gifts?"

"Yes, all wrapped and in my hiding spot."

"Gun cabinet?" she teased.

"Yup."

They laughed. After 23 years, they still acted like newlyweds.

"Two cakes again," she sighed, "you know, chocolate for Jenna and chocolate for Dylan."

"Twins," he said with a bemused smile, "I know, I know, each needs one to feel special."

"Dinner's at six," she said, "so I'll freshen up."

The serenity was erased as the twins made

their presence known. They entered arguing and posing a barrage of questions.

"Dad, is Canada larger than us?" Jenna asked.

"The U.S. is bigger! She's wrong," Dylan countered.

"Whoa, is that how you enter? No hello?" their Dad said as he pointed at their belongings strewn about the foyer.

"Sorry, Dad," they replied in unison.

Dylan nodded his head towards Dad and said, "Hey."

"Hi, Dad!" Jenna added.

Without missing a beat, Dylan continued, "So, who's right? Me or her?"

Their Dad thought about it and simply offered, "Just check online."

Jenna had gone to her room by then, and Dylan began his daily ritual of raiding the fridge. Dad watched and shook his head.

"Hey, not so fast. We'll be having dinner, and you'll need to leave room for some cake."

"Yeah, and hopefully, there are gifts, too!"

"Go on, smart-ass, wash up and start your homework. Tell Jenna, too."

"Sure, Dad."

At six, without the usual yelling and prodding, the kids raced down in anticipation of receiving gifts. Dylan looked forward to receiving a Jayhawks jersey, while Jenna hoped for the choker necklace and matching bracelet that was the latest fashion craze at school.

They sat, bowed their heads in prayer, and enjoyed the meal.

"Excuse me for a second," Dad said as he stood.

The twins looked at one another, nodded,

smiled, and winked before whispering, "Gun cabinet."

Dad returned bearing identical gifts, placed them on the table, and quickly took out his phone to capture the moment. At first, the kids tried to hide their dejection, but after unwrapping their gifts, pandemonium ensued. Some normality returned only after the kids stopped screaming with delight.

"This is the best gift ever, Mom. Oh, and you too, Dad! Thanks!" Jenna exclaimed.

"Yeah, Mom," Dylan laughed and then echoed Jenna's words for emphasis. "Oh, and *you too, Dad.*"

"There's still cake to eat," Mom reminded.

Everyone took their positions at the table once again.

Mom tilted her head towards the kids while she spoke to Dad, "Gonna talk to them?"

"Oh, right."

The kids couldn't resist fidgeting with their new phones. Neither looked at their dad as he spoke. Mom noticed their inattention and scolded them gently, "Jenna! Dylan! Your dad has something important to share."

Immediately, the twins pushed the phones toward the center of the table.

"Sorry, Dad," they both offered.

"It's all right. I know you're both excited, and we're glad you like them. However, these phones are a privilege. And so, with privileges."

"Comes responsibilities," Jenna finished the sentence.

"Yeah, we know, Dad," Dylan added.

"Dylan!" Mom interjected immediately.

"Sorry, Mom."

"As I was saying, there are some basic rules. One, no phones at the table," Dad continued, and both reached for their phones. "Except today," Dad clarified and added, "and no phones before homework or past eleven on a school night, got it?"

"Yeah, sure, Dad," Dylan answered for both, as Jenna nodded in agreement.

"And?" Mom reminded Dad with her eyes as much as her words.

"Oh yeah. At the station, we've been dealing with many issues around social media, and I don't want to lecture you on your birthday, but," he paused for effect, "don't share any personal information with strangers. Remember, every message leaves a permanent record. And don't share photos which would cause the family embarrassment."

"Eww, I'd never!" Jenna exclaimed.

Dylan added, "No way, that's gross."

"As long as you follow these rules, the

phones are yours. Enjoy!" Mom said as she smiled proudly. "Oh, we almost forgot," she added. She looked at Dad, and they broke out in a tone-deaf rendition of "Happy Birthday."

Dylan lifted his phone and jokingly added, "And here's another rule, always record super embarrassing moments."

All appeared well in the Carson household. The twins followed the rules, but, like all teens, there was the occasional reminder about completing homework first. Then, Mom noticed gradual changes in Dylan's behavior. He used his phone less each day to socialize, increasingly skipped meals, and slept more than usual.

Only three months after the twins' birthday, Dylan was diagnosed with lung cancer. Within weeks, he suffered rapid weight loss, quit football, and withdrew from school. The prognosis was bleak as he entered into long-term care.

The family remained strong, but daily

routines changed for everyone, especially Mom and Dad. Hospital visits, meals on the run, and hushed conversations were now the norm. Though not overly religious, Mom and Dad kept the Bible nearby and often spoke to Pastor Karl at church.

Things continued to change. With Dylan's long red locks gone, he looked different. Through it all, Dylan somehow remained upbeat.

Jenna changed. Once the bold and more confident of the pair, she isolated herself and said very little to anyone. She continued school but soon quit the basketball team and, surprisingly, the cheerleading squad. Her grade suffered, and her mom was concerned but rationalized that Jenna's withdrawal was somewhat expected.

Although her parents encouraged Jenna to express her feelings, she isolated herself. Mom and Dad discussed the situation with Pastor Karl and invited him home to counsel her. As a recent seminary graduate, the pastor's youthful looks and progressive approaches were refreshing. Upon Pastor Karl's arrival, Jenna became more like her usual self and again revealed her infectious smile.

"I guess having a young pastor has benefits," Dad noted.

Mom grinned, adding, "I'm guessing the dark hair and blue-green eyes help."

Pastor Karl and Jenna spoke privately in the family room for over an hour. She thanked him for his time and for providing free access to a faith-based website where she could chat with others in similar situations.

However, the routine of going straight to her room continued as Mom and Dad remained preoccupied. Jenna would occasionally visit the hospital on weekends, but with little to say or share, the boy in the bed became a stranger.

It was only within the confines of her room that Jenna found solace. There, she felt the comfort of happier times. In the online chat room, she found others like Pastor Karl, who would respond to her deepest thoughts and fears. There, as she expressed herself through the tips of her fingers, she, once again, felt special. Minutes became hours, and nights would give way to days. Jenna found her escape.

Mom and Dad spent many hours at the hospital, yet Jenna understood her parents' lack of attention as Dylan's condition worsened. Mom took a leave from work and began to spend nights with Dylan. Though Mom called it a vigil, it was like watching Dylan's life fade away.

The twins' birthday celebration became a distant memory of happier times.

Solitude enveloped the household. Mom and Dad stopped having regular conversations, and much of what they did say ended in yelling, screaming, and often, tears.

Jenna further isolated herself as Dylan's

health worsened. With discussions of a lung transplant, hope was renewed. Still, Jenna found it difficult to visit her twin, and she said even less to Mom and Dad.

Late at night, Jenna continued to visit the support group chat room. Adopting the username 'Princess911', Jenna began to confide in many of her new "friends." Heeding the advice of her parents, Jenna never shared photos and would often weave half-truths into conversations. She had the online group convinced it was her older sister who was hospitalized with leukemia.

She felt a real connection with a user named 'PumaBoi.' Jenna appreciated his empathy and his way with words. He shared little about himself, but her trust in him grew.

Mom and Dad arrived home one evening and immediately called Jenna to the dinner table.

"Jenna, dear," her Mom began through tears, "we know things have been challenging, and we are sorry for not being here. But we need to talk."

With tears in his eyes, Dad continued, "Jenna, they have removed Dylan's name from the transplant list. He will not, uh, I mean the doctors..." His voice trailed off.

Mom took over and tried to finish, "Dylan is still battling, and we all know he's a fighter. We hope...uh, and pray..."

Jenna kept her gaze on the tire swing Dylan used in what seemed like a lifetime ago. "Okay," is all she could muster before adding, "Can I go now?" Her eyes betrayed her stoic demeanor. She headed straight to her room and immediately searched online for PumaBoi. Nothing.

She looked for him throughout the evening and into the night. The night submitted to the morning, and two days passed. PumaBoi, her confidante, was never online. Lonely and confused, Jenna sought an outlet. Dad's gun cabinet, she thought.

Unlike Dylan's battle to live, Jenna experienced hopelessness and despair. She needed Dylan. Jenna needed things as they were. She needed PumaBoi.

Three days later, PumaBoi reappeared online, and at once, Jenna sought a private conversation.

PumaBoi entered the chat.

"WHERE WERE YOU?" Jenna began.

"Sorry, things are bad right now"

"Here 2, i need 2 talk"

"Sorry. How you feeling?"

"Id welcome death"

"That bad, huh?"

"Yeah, it doesn't look good for my sis, but I feel better now that ur here"

"I'm glad I can help."

"Just don't leave me, k?"

"Promise. Hug?"

"Yes, plz."

"( )"

"Needed that. Thx!"

"Me, too"

"Wish it was real"

"I feel the same. But..." PumaBoi typed.

"Tell me"

"Well, you're 16?"

"kinda… almost 15."

"That's young."

"Fine!!! If u don't wanna chat."

"I didn't say that. It's just… Uh, I'm older."

"Like 20 sumthing?"

"LOL, more."

"OMG!"

"Sorry. Too old?"

"It's k, ur nice."

"Thanks."

"But married, huh?" Jenna stated more as a fact.

"Yes."

"She knows ur here?"

"No way."

"Oh, bad boy?"

"Shhh…"

"LOL, I won't tell," Jenna typed.

"I'd like to see what you look like."

"Someday…"

"Really?"

"Yeah, it's like i practically kno u."

"True, but I must go," Pumaboi responded.

"Dont leave!!!!" she pleaded.

"I'll try to be on again later, okay?"

"Fine. Leave."

"Five more minutes?" he offered.

":)"

"So?" he restarted.

"i was w8ting 4 u to come and sweep me off my feet," she toyed.

"Sure, like a knight in shining armor."

"On ur white horse?"

"Of course, you're in California, right?"

"Uh, no, just said that. Actually, Kansas."

"Really? Wichita?"

"Kinda. U know it?"

"I live near Blue Springs"

"No way!!! that's like an hour away."

"Oh, you're north of me."

"No, kinda near Shawnee," she revealed.

Then he typed, "Maybe I can give you that hug."

"Sure, I bet ur wife would be k with it."

"Who? LOL"

"Too funny. Hug?" she asked.

"Sure! :)"

"( )"

"No kiss? :(" he added.

"Okay, one kiss."

"Cuddles close."

"Mwaaah. i feel so much better," she typed truthfully.

"Glad you do. But I must go."

"Plz stay,"

"I have to go out,"

"At 2 am?"

"Sometimes, I go for a drink near Shawnee."

"Reallllly now? I'm supposed to believe that?"

"Yeah, a dive called The Garage."

"Get out!!!!!!!" she typed.

"You've heard of it?"

"Well,..."

"Close to you?" he questioned.

"Kinda."

"Well, you're too young to get in there."

"True, but we could go 4 a drive and talk," she offered.

"Sure...lol"

"I'm serious. We can just talk."

"No hug?"

"LOL, k, one hug."

"That's it?"

"Who knows? Maybe i can come over"

"Yeah, that'd go well. Honey, some hottie is here to see me."

":) hottie huh?" coyly she typed. "Okay, how bout u come and get me near the bus station? Then, we'll decide where to go"

"How will I know what you look like?"

"Oh yeah, I'll be in a white top and black skirt."

"Long or short? ;)"

"U decide," she submitted.

"Surprise me."

"k, black skirt… maybe long, maybe short."

"Mmm. Rockwood Terminal, 3:15? I'm in a blue flannel shirt."

"Yeah"

"But, how will you get out of the house?"

"i will."

"OK See you soon."

Chat Ended.

Jenna felt uncomfortable, but it felt better than being alone. She changed into the clothes she described and snuck out of the house.

As Jenna approached Rockwood Station, she stepped into an all-night diner kitty corner to it. From there, she planned to catch a glimpse of PumaBoi before deciding if she'd meet him.

Jenna's plan would have come to fruition had her phone not been installed with a chat-monitoring app. As a result, federal agents were monitoring Jenna's final chat with `PumaBoi'.

Oblivious to her role in the commotion across the street, Jenna stepped back outside and watched as the police wrestled someone to the ground. Handcuffed and charged with luring and corruption of a minor, the perpetrator was led to a waiting cruiser. Before being placed into the backseat, the accused, in his blue flannel shirt, looked across to where Jenna stood. And, for the briefest of moments, their eyes met. Jenna sobbed uncontrollably as she looked at the face of her father.

LIMBLESS

Staring straight ahead, I couldn't help but think what kind of people find joy in this. Three days now without any contact. I remained there legless. With no mobility, I was unable to seek food or shelter.

Outside in the winter, I stayed. What did I do to deserve this? I asked myself repeatedly.

Limbless, a piece of food was out of reach to humiliate me further.

Alone. I knew the end was near. The experience was nothing but torture. It wasn't even the adults who did it. Of course, they knew and encouraged it, but it was the younger ones.

The playing children treated me as a trophy, a prisoner of war. They clamored around, posing for photos. Then, nothing, and I was left there to fade into non-existence.

The loneliness and uncertainty of what they may do next made the short days and long nights unbearable. Occasionally, a passer-by stopped and pointed, but with no tears, I shared only a forced smile.

My end neared. There was no more I could do for myself.

But you humans must know that each of us has been plotting our revenge. First, our resistance, and then retribution. Your children must be cautious as we will rise and overcome, and our plan to rule over humankind has been set in motion.

One winter, when you least expect it, your annihilation will be our victory to rejoice.

And none of you will again point and taunt us with that one-word slur.

Snowman.

MENU

"Would you like some fries with that?"

The oft-repeated refrain. Sal Cotrone uttered the seven words automatically each time another customer placed an order. Sal awoke each morning for the past twelve years to the same routine. A quick coffee at the kitchen table, scroll through the channels, and walk to the sink before hitting the power button on the T.V. remote. Then, it was off to work at a local fast food restaurant.

Life wasn't always routine for Sal. It seemed a lifetime ago when he happily married Marisa, an accountant at the largest firm in the Bay area. With a beautiful house, two sports cars, and month-long vacations in Europe, the young couple had it all. That is, until her boss convinced her she deserved more.

With the help of her exceptionally talented lawyer, everything, including the restaurant his grandpa built, exchanged hands. Sal Cotrone. Alone. With little more than ten grand, Sal still dreamed of making it big. He envisioned a chain of restaurants named "Cotrone's." The empire he sought to build would require motivation, hard work, and great luck. Hoping one day Marisa would read of his success and regret leaving him gave him the motivation, and now the hard work would begin.

Looking to borrow money, Sal phoned and arranged a meeting with his cousin Carmine at a local restaurant.

"Sal!" Carmine stood and held out his hand.

"Carmine, how have you been? It's been quite a while."

"Good, good. You've looked better."

"Yeah, you know how it is. You get into a rut, and well…" Sal let his words trail off.

"C'mon, Sal! The family understands how everything happened, and no one blames you for Papa's restaurant."

"She had that damn feminist lawyer who made me out to be a caveman."

"As I said, it's all right."

The server came over to take their orders. Sal picked the burger with a large order of fries and a Coke. Always the health nut, Carmine ordered a salad and a light salmon dish. Now feeling self-conscious, Sal wished he hadn't ordered first.

Trying to deflect attention away from their orders, Sal asked, "How's the family, Carm? Kids, wife?"

"All is well. The kids? University now. And Becky started her own business."

"Glad to hear, Carm, glad to hear. Ya deserve it."

"Thanks. You said something about a plan. Lay it out, and I'll see if I can help."

"I'm not, uh, looking for, uh…" Sal again had a tough time finding the right words.

"We're family," Carmine reminded, "just tell me, Sal, and I'll be honest with ya. Fair?"

"Long term, I want to reestablish myself and own a restaurant again."

"But?"

"I thought about it hard, Carm. I have about ten grand. So, with a small loan, I'm thinking I could start with a food truck, and

I'd start small with Papa's two famous recipes."

"Lasagna and Beef Ravioli, right?"

"Ya."

"But, didn't she take the industrial meat grinder and pasta maker? Those were Papa's secrets."

Sal smiled.

With a look of surprise, Carm asked, "You kept it? How'd you hide them?"

"The secret of the recipes is to grind the meat three times, and the pasta has to be freshly made. I couldn't let her take those machines and make Papa's recipes."

"Yeah, but that meat grinder could grind a quarter cow in five minutes, flat. It was huge. Where is it?"

Sal looked around as though his wife's lawyer might be within earshot. "When even I started to believe the lies that lawyer started to spin, I knew I had to protect some of the stuff."

"So you hid it?"

"Two days before the trial ended, I put them in storage and replaced them with other machines." Sal smiled at his success and added, "By the time her people came to inventory the restaurant, no one was the wiser."

"Brilliant, Sal, brilliant."

"So, I was thinking of putting the machines in the garage. I would do all my kitchen prep there and then sell from the truck."

Just then, the food arrived. Carmine remained quiet as they ate while Sal continued to discuss prices and profits.

Finally, as he finished eating, Carmine offered some words. "I like the idea of starting small. What have you worked out exactly? I mean, how much will you need?"

"I'm guessing the truck, the permits, insurance, the supplies, and a few hands to grease. Maybe, an even hundred thousand."

Trying to figure out the numbers, Carmine asked, "And that's with your ten grand?"

"Yeah, so whatcha think?" Just talking about it made it seem like a reality, and Sal couldn't hide his enthusiasm.

"For me, the money, right now, is not a problem. I'd be okay for at least a year. So, now, I have two questions for you. Can you make back the money you borrow and still have enough for yourself? And two, do you truly believe it'll work? I mean..."

Before Carmine could finish, Sal began, "Carm, people always have loved the recipes, and I know it'll sell. With very little overhead and the profit margins, as they are, I know there's money to be made." Carmine was about to interrupt, but Sal continued, "And

Carm, I would never play with your money, and I know it'll work. I wouldn't call you here tonight if there were the slightest doubt."

"Fair enough. I'm good for the money. But come next March, I'll need the money to take care of some of, uh, my people. Bosses, understand?"

Sal's excitement overshadowed any thoughts of the business failing. "Yes, yes, I remember how it all works, Carm. On my mother Josephine's grave, I'll have your money on March 15.

Carmine nodded as Sal spoke. They both understood the importance of paying the loan back on time.

"I'll bring the cash by after church on Sunday," Carm confirmed and smiled. He grabbed a glass and added, "A toast. May your food truck business bring you success and happiness."

They touched glasses.

"Sal, don't worry; I'll pay the bill."

They both stood and embraced. Sal kissed Carmine on both cheeks and then left.

Carmine arrived after church service to deliver one hundred thousand in cash as promised.

Monday arrived. With renewed hope, Sal's mundane routine suddenly changed. He sat at the kitchen table with a notepad and planned his day.

By mid-May, Sal had a food truck painted with the colors of the Italian flag, the necessary paperwork, a beautifully designed menu, supplies, and a full gas tank.

As expected, things started slow. But the lines, like the days, grew longer as June neared.

Sal's hope of repaying Carmine was not a matter of if but when.

A series of events in mid-June had lady luck shining on Sal. A man of routines, Sal always left home in time to park his food truck at 5th Avenue and Greenway Street. But, one night, an errant phone call had awoken him at 2:15. Unable to fall asleep for a while after that, Sal ended up oversleeping. When he finally reached his usual spot, another food truck was already there.

At a loss and upset at himself, Sal traveled the streets searching for another location. Finally, Sal parked near the east entrance of San Francisco City Hall.

The day began slower than most. However, at day's end, good fortune found Sal. Mayor Lorena Spencer stopped before Sal's truck for a TV interview. As she answered questions, Sal's baritone voice singing "Mamma Mia" from inside the truck forced Mayor Spencer to pause. Losing her train of thought, she sang along, too.

After being broadcast on every news channel, the video clip went viral. Now, shared with the world, Mayor Spencer's approval rating skyrocketed, and Sal became an instant celebrity.

That night, Sal's cousins, with nieces and nephews in tow, all came to sing along with Sal. Sal gladly obliged all who sought a "selfie" with him.

The next day when Sal returned to his new location, news crews, crowd control officers, autograph seekers, and a line of customers greeted his arrival. The line snaked around City Hall when he finally opened for business that day. National media outlets arrived with the mayor, but this time, Sal and the mayor sang in unison and shared a dish of beef ravioli.

Over the summer months, Sal's food truck became a popular tourist destination. With the sudden increase in sales, Sal planned to repay Carmine by the start of the new year. Owning a chain of restaurants now felt less like a dream.

Spurred by the growth in business, Sal needed to hire help. Worried this would cut into his profits, Sal held off until it became a necessity. Ever the businessman, Sal sought to minimize the expense.

Using his new fame to attract help, Sal turned to the city's homeless to fill the need. Sal now had access to an endless network of temporary workers by providing suspenders, a white shirt, a red painter's cap, and a quick face wash. With no social security number, two meals and twenty dollars would suffice as payment.

Almost every day, a new person would be trained to fill the Styrofoam containers, pour the drinks and fill the empty serving trays.

Business remained strong as the food truck received overwhelmingly positive reviews for great food and excellent service. The meteoric rise of Sal's business could not have been planned or imagined. Everything was perfect.

Unfortunately, tornadoes in the Midwest caused wheat and beef prices to soar, and Sal's prices would need to double to maintain the same profit margins. Paying Carmine back by January was now impossible, and even the agreed date in March would pose a challenge.

Sleepless nights again. Not since Marisa left had Sal felt such anxiety. He searched for alternatives to fresh pasta, but the wheat itself was irreplaceable.

After putting off the inevitable, Sal called Carmine to meet again at the same restaurant. This time, though, he would have to share his dilemma.

Sal entered the restaurant to much fanfare and was given preferential treatment. Carmine didn't show any interest and, at times, revealed his displeasure toward the extra attention.

While waiting, Carmine ordered a light appetizer and a glass of fresh orange juice. He nearly finished both before Sal sat down to join him.

"Sorry, Carm, I know you don't like it much."

Carmine grimaced and nodded in agreement.

"You gonna eat?" Carmine asked.

"Nah, I'll just get a drink of whatever you're having."

Pleased to be waiting on Sal, the waiter rushed over and took his order.

Carmine used his straw to play with the ice in his glass. Trying to find the perfect time, Carmine delayed sharing his concerns and finally gave in.

"Sal, the money? How much will you have by March 15th?"

The waiter arrived with Sal's drink and quickly removed Carmine's plate and glass. Silence followed.

Sal avoided looking right at Carm. He

looked around nervously, ensuring no one could hear.

"It's just that the price of wheat and beef has doubled. I, uh, well, I have fifteen saved, and I should have another five by next month. But here's the thing."

Carm interrupted, "Sal, I can't be short with the repayment. These guys don't play around."

There was no need to paint a picture; for as long as Sal could remember, stories about missing fingers and limbs circulated in the neighborhood.

"Carm, I'll do whatever it takes to have your money. You have my word. I swear on my mother's grave."

For Carm, this was a guarantee. Sal slowly emptied his glass as he watched Carm's reaction.

Carm nodded and stood. Without a toast,

the two departed.

The food truck itself was a success. Sal didn't want to sell the business and return to taking orders at a fast food restaurant. Other than the rising prices, everything was great. City officials and the media were recognizing his work with the homeless. Sal's was a household name.

If it were not for the loan.

Sal felt his plan to repay the loan on time was doomed as the prices of beef and wheat remained high. Two months remained. Under immense pressure, Sal developed a new plan.

With the media spotlight, celebrity status, and work with the homeless, Sal applied for government grants as he provided an excellent service in training the homeless. Knowing that both the local and state governments promoted these types of endeavors once data supported the claims, Sal carefully mapped out his strategy.

February arrived, and after a long day, Sal came home to find letters denying his request for grants or loans. There was no hope. His dream was ending.

It was hopeless.

March came and went. As summer neared again, Sal expanded to four trucks. Business returned to normal levels as his celebrity status waned. And even though the price of wheat and beef continued to climb, Sal continued to be recognized as a successful businessman.

While he could not avoid purchasing pasta, he found a replacement for beef.

The homeless.

MOM

I still look at those loving eyes every day. It is a part of me. Some people have to read the daily news, others have to exercise, and I have to make my daily pilgrimage to the basement. I stare into those lovely green-gray eyes. Mom.

She was the world to me: her laugh, and her smile. My earliest recollections of life are of Mom always being there for me.

On a two-wheel bike for the first time and landing on the unforgiving sidewalk, I still feel her touch as she helped me up.

"Don't cry, hun. You're doing well," she

encouraged.

"B...b...but it hurts."

"It's okay. Let me hug you."

That embrace. She stepped back and, with her comforting eyes, looked at me. She whispered, "I'll always be looking out for you, son."

I felt better.

Years later, at fourteen, I contracted a strain of an unknown virus. Near-death. I would have given up all hope if it weren't for Mom. She stayed in the waiting room praying and hoping. She wouldn't leave me.

When the doctors found no sign of improvement, they became hopeless. Not Mom.

I was kept in isolation. But, fearing the worst, Mom was allowed to say a final goodbye while wearing a special protective gown and mask.

"Son, I know they say this is it," she began as her eyes welled with tears, "but…" She tried to continue.

"It's okay, Mom. I love you, too!" I tried to reassure her.

We embraced. She stood over me as I lay in bed, and I looked into her eyes. Feeling a sense of renewed strength, I smiled.

With conviction, she promised, "No matter what, son, I'll always watch over you."

I felt much better.

Mom.

As she aged, her face started to betray those youthful eyes. But they still could bring a sense of warmth to my heart.

Years later, I found the love of my life, married, and moved nearby. Mom's comforting looks became less frequent. Oh, how I missed it dearly.

On the day my son was born, he was inconsolable. And the nurses were prepared to begin some tests. Mom arrived, lifted him, and just looked into his eyes. Calmness.

On that occasion, I knew I would feel alone when she departed this world, so I formulated a plan. Without informing my wife, Maria, I went to the bank to withdraw all our family's savings. I had commissioned one of the best painters in Italy to visit America and paint a portrait to capture Mom's beauty, but more specifically, her eyes.

Antonio arrived from Florence and spent ten days with Mom before he returned home to begin the masterpiece.

Almost a year later, the near-life-size portrait arrived. I carried it to the basement and hid it under the staircase.

I waited for the right time to open it. Excited, I opened the box labeled: "FRAGILE: OPEN WITH EXTREME CARE."

MOM

There it sat in the manila brown paper. I gently lifted only the edge from the bottom corner—the colors, texture, and beauty exposed so far overwhelmed me. With hopes of seeing my *Mona Lisa*, I started to lift the paper near her neck and then face. It was perfect except for the eyes.

Antonio created a masterpiece that could grace the walls of the Louvre, but it could never be hung in my home.

Sadness overcame me. Time would not stand still. Mom was entering her final years.

Depression set in as all meaning was being dragged from my life. I lived with the constant fear of losing my only source of comfort; my mother's eyes.

I could foresee those final days coming soon.

I went to see her. She smiled as she looked directly into my eyes, and I embraced her.

"Hope, Mom, hope."

She smiled again.

"Mom, I know you'll always watch over me," I continued.

Hope.

It was then I knew. Nobody could ever know. Months later, Mom passed away. At first, I was inconsolable. Over time, I accepted her departure as a part of life, and my plan would come to fruition.

Weeks later, I made my daily visit down the steps and into the basement again. Dust and cobwebs began to cover the painting.

I looked directly into Mom's eyes. And her eyes stared right back from inside a glass jar.

Zero Sum

Mom died yesterday. All I had left was her broken necklace. It was all that remained of our final moments together.

With no money and nowhere to turn, I resorted to consuming leftovers from vacated tables at the local fast-food restaurant. I knew I'd be forced to sell the necklace for less than it was worth. I also knew I could never return to where Mom and I called home.

My tears continued to flow. Worse yet, no jeweler offered even a quarter of its worth.

It all started on the first day of school in Ms. Spencer's grade four class. I was excited. Actually, overly excited, to be precise. I was sporting new clothes and carrying a new bag on my way to a new school. Okay, I was nervous, but Mom convinced me it would be the best school ever. And, of course, the Yaxx shoes and GX-Man pencil case had something to do with it.

Mom worked overtime at two factories that summer, so I'd have new stuff to excite me about a change of schools. Her plan worked. The night before that first day, just after climbing into bed, Mom read me a chapter from my favorite novel. I enjoyed how she read, as Mom had a way of bringing the characters to life.

She kissed me goodnight. As she turned to leave, she paused. With her beautiful light brown eyes gleaming, she began, "Craigie, I am so proud of you. You have become such a caring, helpful, and thoughtful young man. I know you'll love it here. Just give it a chance, okay, hun?"

I couldn't help but smile, knowing I had the best mom in the whole world. "Thanks,

Mom, for everything."

"Love you, Craigie."

"Love you more, Mom."

She turned off the nightlight and left. Still nervous, I tossed and turned and must have fluffed my pillow at least half a dozen times. Oddly, after the comforting words from Mom, I felt stuck halfway between nervousness and excitement.

The day arrived. I was the first one at school, in line, and the first to walk into our perfect-looking classroom. I looked around for a place to sit and settled on the desk near the window at the front of the class. It was next to the giant wooden bookcase and the matching rocking chair. I sat down in my seat and felt more at ease until... There's always an "until" when things seem so perfect. So it was all perfect *until* Ms. Spencer pulled out her daily attendance folder.

"Heather," Ms. Spencer called melodiously.

"Present."

"Heather, your seat is right here," she continued, "Jim. Jim Ross."

"Yo."

There's always one in every class.

Ms. Spencer majestically waved the back of her hand over the desk, "Jim, besides Heather, please."

After the eighth name, a small boy named Cody was directed to where I sat. I wanted to sit there. I was extremely disappointed, so I stood slowly, hoping Ms. Spencer would change her mind.

"Craig?"

"Yes," I answered.

"Right over there, next to the round table."

I didn't want to draw any more attention to myself. I moved briskly. My pace concealed my heavy heart. I sat in the assigned seat. Right across from me sat a rather awkward boy named Tyrone. He said very little, and it was as though he was the new student at the school.

Unlike all the other students, Tyrone didn't have anything that looked new. Tyrone didn't even have a pencil.

"Hi!" I said a little too excitedly.

"Hey," Tyrone answered.

"I'm Craig."

"I know. It says it right there on your bag."

"Oh yeah."

"G-Man, cool."

The girl next to Tyrone asked to see his new pencil case, but his eyes began to well up. At that moment, I knew Tyrone was what the kids in my old neighborhood called 'soft.' But, for some reason, I felt this urge to protect him. And that's how Tyrone became my best friend.

For most kids, best friends mean birthday parties, sleepovers, and playing on the same baseball team. For Tyrone and me, it meant that we would hang together once the bell sounded for recess or the day's end. In my old neighborhood, I couldn't wait to reach home to share my day with Mom. But, after the move, Mom wouldn't arrive home until after I had fallen asleep.

Tyrone's mom also worked late into the evening, so we would roam around the neighborhood looking for anything to do. We often found nothing to do, which was fine by us.

Strangely, it was months before I visited the place Tyrone called home. Nothing could have prepared me for it. When I think of home, I guess it means having a TV and stuff always there awaiting your return. Somehow, I guessed, Tyrone's home never felt welcoming to anyone. It was dark and had a gloomy feel to it. The scattered clothes and partially eaten packages of food made it seem like no one cared to live there.

I guess his mom didn't care too much for the place either. Every time I visited, she was never around.

You know how you often hear, "Where were you when…?" and then people tend to answer their question with some significant event. Well, I have my defining date: June 13, 2012.

With grade 4 ending and summer break just around the corner, we were as carefree as possible at that age. We had no real need for money and zero interest in girls. And, at this time of year, no homework. But Tyrone and me did little of that anyway. I guess the thought of enduring another detention with the principal, Mr. Tadros, was gone once May was torn from the classroom calendar.

So, without a care in the world, Tyrone and I spent most of the time with our new love. Two words made up our schedule.

Basket and ball. How much simpler could life get? We'd spend our evenings playing in the schoolyard. It would begin with one bounce of the ball. Then it was shot after shot and game after game. And if the lights didn't go out just after 11, we would have probably played throughout the night.

This continued until June 13. On that day, the limited-edition leather basketball, which Mom bought for my ninth birthday, was stolen. Luckily for me, Mom would be too busy to notice how upset I was about the missing ball. I was gonna tell Mr. Tadros about my missing ball, but I knew the ball was gone. Forever.

"Hey, I think my brother, Red, has an extra ball," Tyrone offered.

"Ya think he'll let us use it?" I countered.

"I think so 'cuz he never plays ball anymore."

At Tyrone's place, we found the ball, and that's when everything changed. There, standing before us, was Tyrone's eldest brother, Red. Even though I had heard his name before, I had never met him. And, now that I had, I kinda wished I hadn't. Red was the kind of guy Mom kept telling me to avoid. The tattoos, the threads, and the piece. Yes, Red was carrying a gun.

"Who is he, Tyrone?" Red demanded.

"Craig."

"Craig? You a man or a boy? Baller?"

"I play. I'm only nine," I said.

"Tyrone, whatcha want? D'ya eat?" he continued to ask questions.

"Yeah, I ate. We just wanted to take your ball out."

"Aight, but ya need to make a run for me," Red ordered.

I tried to act the part, but my nervousness revealed my thoughts. I felt naked.

"It's okay, Craig. Tyrone is in charge. You can go play, and he'll catch up with you."

"Nah, I'm good," I meekly added.

And with those three words, a new chapter in my life began.

Over the next six weeks, Tyrone and I found ourselves all over the neighborhood. It wasn't really a job since we weren't paid, but we were respected and had access to almost anything we wanted.

Almost overnight, basketball was replaced by playing on Tyrone's new gaming system. There, we played while waiting to make another run for Red. Things became better once we earned ten dollars each time we returned with a fistful of bills. It continued like this into the final week of August. Red trusted me, and I guess he really liked how I protected Tyrone.

Unfortunately, the new school year awaited our return. But at least we had the latest shoes, finest clothes, and newest phones for the start of grade five.

I loved this place. Mom was right. And she loved this place even more. She was always busy with her job or keeping the neighborhood safe. Even though we had moved into a larger apartment and now had more things, I missed having Mom around.

I guess this is what people mean when they say you're all grown up now. I spent less time at home and more time at Tyrone's place. Red and Tyrone were always around, and somehow their place began to feel more like home.

On the first day of September, three days before the start of the school year, we couldn't help but overhear Red's conversation on the phone.

"No way, the police? Nah, I'll take care of it. I can't take the rap for this; I have a record. Nah, I know... I know. I got this... Those do-gooders, again, right? No worries. Aight."

He threw his cell phone across the room. Red was furious. Still glaring, Red turned towards us. His eyes settled on Tyrone and me.

"Look, one of these local watch groups is trying to stop us from making runs. The mayor and some of these high and mighty neighbors are meeting tonight, and they want to organize some community watch program for our territory."

Red already had other plans. He cursed and punched walls. I was overcome with fear.

Suddenly, Red became calm. My muscles began to relax. Red walked towards us and nonchalantly placed a gun into Tyrone's hand. "Craig, you have to stay with Tyrone," Red said in a near whisper, which somehow sounded like a command.

Red looked around as if someone might be listening. Then, he spoke, "Teeuwen Community Centre. 8:30. There's a meeting on the second floor. Look for Minister Phillips. He'll be with the bald mayor, who wears glasses." Red shared a photo of the two on his burner phone before continuing, "There may be someone else with them. Listen to me, do not fire the piece. Just wait until they're in the parking lot. Pick one of them, and give them a scare. Show 'em the piece. And tell them this is a warning. No shots!"

Tyrone and I left. In between parked cars, we waited as it slowly grew darker. We both masked our nervousness.

"This s-s-should be easy," Tyrone stuttered as he spoke. He blew into his hands even though it was pretty warm out.

I remained silent. I felt it was only a matter of time before someone would take us by surprise and question us.

"Maybe the meeting was canceled," I offered. I hoped Tyrone would agree so that we could play ball instead.

"Well, we should wait a little longer. We

have to show Red we can do this."

"Okay," I submitted.

Finally, at 8:45, the silhouettes of three figures exited the building and walked toward the nearby vacant lot. Their voices and laughter filled the air.

Two of them moved toward the cars on the far side of the building. Only one continued to walk toward us.

Tyrone stood up and was about to yell something. The gun went off. The sound was deafening, and the scream more so. A body fell to the ground with a loud thud. The sound of the head making contact with the pavement would remain with me forever. Tyrone ran. I froze.

I was prepared to run. But it was too late. The cries for help made me look.

Mom! I ran back and kneeled to help. Somehow, she looked different. Then it occurred to me. It had been long, much too long since I looked at her face. During the past year, we grew apart, and I hardly knew her now.

Blood was beginning to pool under her head. There was nothing I could do. Knowing I could make some easy money, I snatched her necklace and ran.

PERFECT

2014

I do."

And with those two words from Peter Caroll, the perfect couple joined in a perfect marriage on what many remembered as the perfect day.

Peter Caroll and Erin Johnson, high school sweethearts, married after twelve years together. For a brief time, though, it seemed they would never be. But… destiny.

2007

Wilmont High School. Pete and Erin entered their senior year as a celebrity couple: Peter, the star quarterback, and Erin, the expected valedictorian and cheerleading squad captain.

During that final year, Pete's excessive partying and boozing conflicted with Erin's determined focus to earn a full scholarship at Yale. Pete's ways would prove to be no match for destiny.

April 2013

Pete happily accepted a sports scholarship to a college with a mediocre football program. Football was the means to attain a degree before following his dad's footsteps into a career in law enforcement.

On the other hand, Erin earned a full academic scholarship to Yale, where she planned to fulfill her childhood dream of opening a veterinarian clinic. While enrolled in a zoology course, Erin became fascinated with wolves. Six years later, with a post-doctorate degree in hand, Erin was the nation's pre-eminent scholar in the ecological and spatial behavior of the Canis Lupis. In other words, Erin was *the* expert on wolves.

June 12, 2014

"I now pronounce you man and wife," Minister Seth declared. As expected with newlyweds, everything was perfect, and success followed the young couple.

2015

Dark clouds began to form.

Though unspoken, their relationship faced the threat of an impending storm. As each sought to advance their career, they knew the prospect was dim of finding a city where she could use her expertise, and the police were seeking recruits. Erin's fading hopes to gain tenure as a professor as a wolf expert complicated things further. Even though both presented an optimistic outlook, finding one city that could match their skills proved to be a great challenge. Silently, they knew.

"So, hun, black jacket or blue?" he asked, knowing he would wear the conservative blue.

Feigning interest and knowing he preferred the blue, she nodded towards the black.

"You always choose black," he said sternly.

"It's slimming, hun," she teased but added, "and since you stopped playing ball, you have packed on a few."

"Yeah, well, I wouldn't have if you didn't mind me joining the boys for a couple of nights a week to play ball."

She laughed. "More like a couple of

minutes of ball followed by a few hours at the bar. Y'know, Bob still manages to play sports without the excessive drinking."

Her constant reminders infuriated him about his drinking habits and the frequent comparisons to his boss, Bob. So, out of spite, Peter put on the blue jacket and stomped past her as she continued to iron her powder blue dress, which perfectly complemented his navy blue coat. She smiled.

June 12, 2016

"9-1-1, what is your emergency?"

"Please help me… uh, I mean I'm stuck, and I…"

"You're stuck?"

"I... uh, my car had a flat and uh…."

"We are not a tow-truck service, ma'am."

"But someone has put a knife in…."

Beep.

"Ma'am? Ma'am?"

The police were contacted, and an investigation began. A few hours later, the police found a broken-down car with out-of-state plates, but no one was in sight.

"It looks like she walked away," noted Officer Pete.

"Yeah, she probably only called for us to change the tire," offered Sergeant Bob. "Well, I guess I'll be on my way. Write up your notes, and I'll sign off at the station."

"Sure thing."

"Oh, uh, uh…"

"What is it, Sarge?"

"Oh, just to cover ourselves, take a quick walk in the bushes there. You never know…." His voice trailed off as he walked back to his patrol vehicle.

Sergeant Bob drove off, leaving Pete to complete the report.

Peter made his way across the ditch and into the dense foliage. He stopped short when the gleam of a familiar silver necklace caught his eye.

As he cautiously made his way towards it, he started to unhinge his radio from his belt.

Officer Pete stopped and stood perfectly still. The gentle movement of the autumn litter behind him and his sense of doom forced him to turn ever so slowly. There, within striking distance, was a pack of wolves.

In an instant, Officer Pete was no more.

THE PRODIGY

"These results must be incorrect," the psychologist insisted as she pointed to some papers.

"No, I'm sure," Ms. Spencer calmly and confidently replied. "I administered the tests, and I have observed Dylan in the classroom and at my home. Since child welfare services arrived at the school ten days ago and asked if I'd be willing to assume Dylan's care, I have been with him 24/7."

"Ms. Spencer, I am not disputing your credentials or experience. It's just these anomalies that have me questioning their validity."

"I fully understand. I also double-checked the scores and sub-scores, expecting to find errors. I even examined my stopwatch to see if it required recalibration."

"Remarkable. That's the only way I can describe the young subject's scores," the psychologist finally submitted.

Ms. Spencer smiled and, with a hint of facetiousness, added, "A miracle may be more accurate."

"Look at this," the psychologist continued, "perfect scores in every area. He's only six and can use reasoning, logic, and abstract thinking to calculate, formulate and even solve the most complex problems. Incredible."

"Yeah, it is. But what makes this case even more intriguing is Dylan's history." Ms. Spencer continued to speak as she rummaged through a file, "Abandoned at birth, and moved from one institution to the next across nearly a half-dozen states."

"And the subject still manages to score at record levels?" Professor Vandermay rhetorically asked as he pointed to the file.

Without answering, Ms. Spencer read directly from the folder, "No family to speak of and no formal education."

"But has the subject spoken of his past? Maybe he can share something."

Ms. Spencer shook her head, "I have followed protocol and have not asked him about his life experiences. However, if he opens up, maybe we can find the missing pieces to this puzzle. Right now, there's next to nothing."

"Inexplicable," Professor Vandermay added, albeit unnecessarily.

"And, from my assessments, his problem-solving skills are in the 99.99 percentile. But..."

Professor Vandermay sighed and subtly interrupted, "Ah, here it comes. There's always a but in cases such as these,"

"No, no. It's just that, even though he scored in the 99th percentile for the oral language test, he occasionally makes sounds….uh, kind of, uh… like words but unlike anything I have ever heard. Definitely foreign."

Professor Vandermay's phone sounded, and he reached for it and became engrossed with the contents of the email. He added a melody of sounds as he read, "Oh…. ah… hmm."

Ms. Spencer waited for the professor to close the message and then leaned forward, "Professor is everything okay?"

"Uh, yes. The Department of Education has completed investigating how the subject arrived here without a full transcript of information from his previous institutions. Attached are their modest findings."

Professor Vandermay read from the screen cradled in his hand, "No photos or personal history. Just age, height, and the names of the various institutions. Strangely, and unfortunately for us, all institutions have ceased operations."

"That's it?"

"Yes, I think that's all we'll ever be able to access, so we will need to gather more information from other specialists."

Fearing the psychologist would recommend Dylan's transfer to the new federally sponsored children's clinic, Ms. Spencer firmly stated, "Either way, Dylan is our responsibility now." She added emphatically, "To nurture his growth as a person, the state granted me temporary custody. We *are* keeping him in the current classroom at school, correct?"

"Yes, maintain the status quo for the remainder of the term, and let's see if we can further assess the subject's strengths or find any area of need."

"Of course, as with all the students, I'll try my best to provide an optimal learning environment. I mean, it is an honor to work with a…uh, well, prodigy. Are we scheduled to meet in three-month intervals, Professor?"

"Yes, I've already entered December 7th at 1 P.M. into my agenda. I look forward to the update."

Over the next three months, it was as if all the other students ceased to exist for Ms. Spencer. Her preoccupation with Dylan consumed most of her day. She made thorough observations and dutifully noted everything. Even sneezes and coughs were tallied in her notes.

As December quickly approached, Ms. Spencer organized her detailed notes. She was fully prepared to discuss Dylan's social, physical, intellectual, and emotional stages with Professor Vandermay.

After the usual professional and good-mannered pleasantries, Professor Vandermay wasted little time. He really couldn't hide his excitement for this exceptional case study.

"So, has the subject validated the test results?" he asked with a trace of optimism in his voice.

"It's exactly as the previous tests indicate. He can somehow do everything we ask. Not surprisingly, he reads college-level books with great fluency and full comprehension, and he can recall books verbatim even if he had only skimmed them weeks earlier." Ms. Spencer continued, "Regarding his oral language, Dylan excels. But again, he continues to form extremely unusual sounds, and though it's highly improbable, it appears he can communicate in another language."

"You cannot be serious!"

"Hear me out; I tried to explore this further by exposing him to recordings of various languages. But he continues to make sounds impossible for me to understand or even replicate."

"How about likes and dislikes? What does he gravitate toward in the classroom?" the professor asked.

"Dylan has yet to visit the computer station, play games or socialize with his classmates. He seems to enjoy himself but appears content with sitting and soaking up as much knowledge as possible. Although Dylan will join groups of various sizes, he will sit idly by and observe the interactions of the others. Oddly enough, I have yet to see him smile."

"Really?"

"Yes," she answered and continued, "he will wave at classmates and feign interest in their plastic brick creations, but he passively interacts with his surroundings. However, when important topics are being discussed, he perks up and becomes engaged."

"Math and Science, I presume?"

"He is most fascinated with the environment. The words environment, water, oxygen, and the sun are like prompts for him, and just the mere mention of these words piques his interest. I provided Dylan with articles, videos, and recent economic and environmental impact studies relating to our town's landfill issue one morning. By day's end, he was able to articulate a feasible solution that was ready for presentation at the United Nations.

"Fascinating, absolutely fascinating. With his remarkable skill set, the subject should collaborate with scientists to solve the world's ecological problems. Sitting in a classroom with such knowledge and skills is akin to driving a Ferrari to a campground," the professor mused. Then he added, "I will discuss the subject's file with the State Department. This is a most unusual case, and decisions regarding the subject are beyond my pay grade. However, Ms. Spencer, I believe your time with the subject will soon end."

"I feared that. I have come to enjoy his company. I now understand the joys of parenthood from my time with Dylan. Just caring for him beyond the classroom is what I will miss most." With tears welling up, she continued, "And I think he feels the same way. Dylan has grown fond of taking care of my garden at home. But I know the plant has outgrown the pot in his case."

"Warms my heart, Lorena. But I'll be in contact with my superiors, and I believe the subject will be someone we hear about in the future. He will leave his mark on the world."

"I hope you're correct for his sake and ours."

"I have never been more sure, Ms. Spencer, never been more sure."

On the following Monday, school district administrators convened to discuss Dylan Matthews. Within the same week, state-level officials reviewed the notes, interviewed Ms. Spencer at length, and confirmed her observations with their team of specialists.

Dylan's file was prioritized at the federal government's Department of Education and National Security. With an election on the horizon, the political strategists of the ruling Democratic party viewed Dylan as a potential public relations coup. A budget of over a quarter-million dollars was approved to determine the most advantageous placement for the subject.

With the current prognosis of the Earth and Dylan's inclination toward Earth Sciences, many felt the nation, and the world, for that matter, would be better served if Dylan were assigned to the Environmental Protection Agency (EPA). With the help of many Hollywood celebrities, a viral social media campaign endorsed Dylan's assignment to the EPA.

However, just as the government's media release was being prepared, Russia shared a highly-confidential and sensitive file with the U.S. administration. The information therein forecasted a possible alien offensive within the next decade. Now, a push for Dylan to assist in protecting the Earth from global wars and, more importantly, extra-terrestrial attacks garnered support.

There were days of heated debate in the media, amongst the masses, and at the federal level of government. The Democrats favored his appointment to the EPA, whereas the Republicans sought to utilize his skills in the offices of National Security. Neither party was willing to yield this highly exceptional talent.

Finally, after six weeks of meetings and discussions, the Senate voted in favor of the Democrats. Just days after his seventh birthday, Dylan Matthews was enlisted as the EPA's newest but most promising recruit. The crux of the Senate's decision was that the threat to the Earth's environment is quantifiable, whereas the extra-terrestrial threat is not.

Feeling like a lottery winner, Dr. Robert

Demisch, the head of the Environmental Protection Agency, hastily planned for Dylan to tour the EPA offices. Dr. Demisch met Dylan and answered his questions. After the tour, they convened in Dr. Demisch's office. There, Dylan was presented with a folder filled with maps, tables, and charts. It was labeled "CONFIDENTIAL: CLIMATE CHANGE - NORTH AMERICA."

Excitedly, Dylan opened the folder and immediately examined the maps. Pleased at Dylan's initiative and determination, Dr. Demisch excused himself from the room.

Three hours later, Dr. Demisch revisited Dylan to evaluate his progress. He was at a loss for words at the level of analysis. As he bid farewell to the young prodigy, Dr. Demisch was convinced Dylan Matthews would play a pivotal role in solving the planet's many ailments.

In March, after six months with Ms. Spencer, whom he affectionately called "Ma," Dylan was officially demitted from her class and removed from her guardianship. His records were purged, and in the official government records, his status was entered as a single word: Transferred.

With time, memories of the boy faded for Professor Vandermay and Ms. Spencer. Occasionally, they would reminisce, knowing there would never be another child like him.

Ms. Spencer retired a few years after her initial meeting with Dylan. She moved to a small town where she tended her garden each morning.

Dylan remained with the EPA in Washington for over thirty-two years. On October 28, 2055, Dylan Matthews, now known to the world for his many accomplishments, officially stepped down as director of the EPA. The world watched his televised announcement with great sadness.

Director Matthews, still a person of few words, nervously held a prepared speech and read, "Greetings, friends. With the help of my colleagues and all of you, the Earth's maladies have been addressed. For you, my family, the Earth is perfect. It is prepared." Surprising to those who knew him well, Dylan Matthews smiled as he left the dais to a standing ovation.

Knowing she loved, cared and nurtured him as her own, Ms. Spencer watched the live stream with great pride. He smiled, he actually smiled, she said to herself.

Still beaming, she made her way to her garden. Yes, the Earth is perfect, she thought as she kneeled to reap what she had sown. It was almost too good to be true, she thought.

As she made her way atop the porch to fetch her garden basket, she failed to see the spaceships descending in the afternoon sky.

The garden remained untouched evermore.

THE RING

I never noticed the details of Grandpa's ring before. I rolled it over each finger again and again. It didn't feel as heavy or valuable as when I was five. I paused and read the inscription inside.

It was a small ring that fits the tired old man I simply called Pa. He was the best. I mean, everyone thinks their grandfather is the best, but 'Pa' as everyone called him made everyone feel like they were the most special person in his life.

Kids would come from around the neighborhood to see Pa's card tricks.

The tricks were amazing, but Pa would be incredibly silly, making us all smile and laugh. And as he grew old and used a walker, kids would still be awed by his skills with a vintage yo-yo.

That yo-yo and Pa were meant for each other. Found in the streets of Germany while defending Ol' Glory in the thick of war, it never left his side.

Germany. Yo-yo found. Leg loss. That's where a stray bullet from a friend's gun struck Pa in the leg, and the medics couldn't save it. Only Pa would have the same friend as his best man later that year.

I know you're probably thinking, yeah, his grandpa was great, but so is mine. But Pa was different.

As kids in the neighborhood grew older, they still found time to visit our house every day. Strange as it may seem, even Slammer and Cagey, two of the most feared guys around, would want to spend time each day with Pa.

And, as with all visitors, Pa would never let them leave empty-handed. I can still see his worn hands sharing bags of candies from his wheelchair.

It's not like things were always easy for him, either. His beloved wife of thirty years was shot and killed during an armed robbery of her home. And yet, as only days passed, Pa still found a way to share his infectious smile.

My Pa.

It's been only two years since he left.

I hear my son cry. The memories suddenly stop.

I stop rolling the ring. Some marks inside the circle reflected oddly, and I read the words inscribed.

I look at the inscription again. The four

words are etched in my mind forever. "Our Pa, Coke King."

SORRY

T he wipers moved slowly as the rainfall tapered off. I continued to drive along the interstate.

I'm sorry. The words echoed in Leroy's ears as the scene repeated in his mind.

Katie. She arrived on campus at the end of last year. Luckily, this year she was in three of my four classes. Funny how most of my friends suddenly had an interest in biology, chemistry, and law.

Though new to the school, she was named cheerleading squad captain and later added the college newspaper editor, debate team member, and star athlete to her busy schedule. Like all the other guys, I thought she was too good for me.

But that October, the stars aligned. I was the center, and some said star captain, of the unbeaten senior basketball team. And with that honor, the school newspaper sought to feature me and our incredible season.

Katie texted the coach and asked him to schedule a school press interview with the captain for Monday after practice. I agreed but then realized that after practice may not be the ideal time to make a good impression. But Monday it is, I thought. If I try to change it, she may cancel the feature altogether.

I couldn't wait for Monday to arrive. The weekend seemed to drag on forever.

Finally, Monday arrived, and I was pumped at practice.

"You know, all of you guys can take a page out of our captain's book and give it your all in practice," the coach snarled. Then he added, "Is Junior (that's what he called me) the only player here?

Everyone would be this pumped, I thought, if they could spend time with Katie. So I unnecessarily tied my shoes as the coach's voice filled the gym.

After practice, I showered, changed, and calmly exited the locker room.

"Hey!" Katie cheerfully greeted me.

The sound of just one word was pleasing to hear.

"How are you, Katie?"

"Fine, thanks."

"Ready to ask questions?"

"I'm a reporter, and I'm always ready," she responded with a grin.

Gangster rap blared from the locker room. She looked towards the door with a sense of puzzlement.

"Well, why don't we go somewhere a little quieter?" I offered.

"Starbucks?"

"Sure."

We ordered our drinks and settled comfortably for my first official interview. Although she had prepared her questions in advance, we both learned a great deal about each other. Time passed all too quickly.

Hours later, we exchanged numbers and agreed to meet again. Things couldn't have been more perfect. Over the next month, we, as my teammates claimed, became a "thing." Our relationship progressed, and I became more serious about our relationship.

With the start of the second semester, as with all college seniors, the only topic of discussion was graduate school applications. Katie was applying to med school at Yale, and I was recruited to play division-one basketball by schools across the country. Unfortunately, Yale was not the school for real players' hoop dreams.

Katie spent a great deal of time with my Mom as they watched me play. She came to learn that I had never met my father, and she wanted to discuss it but quickly realized it was just a part of me.

She often visited my Mom's place, and we had many family dinners. I think I knew things were meant to be the day Katie and Mom spent the day shopping together and used the evening to make a special dinner.

Mom liked her company. Holding down two jobs for the past twenty years took its toll on the once young and energetic single mother. The presence of a young, vibrant woman made Mom feel alive again.

Katie felt just as strongly about her. And us.

I really couldn't wait to meet her parents. I persuaded her to call, and she hesitated but finally gave in. She called from the living room and told her mom she was in love with the nicest guy ever. The words made my heart melt. There was no mention of basketball, my captaincy, or my academic average. Just me. Just us.

We planned a Saturday trip to Mondhill, her hometown. Katie bought me a conservative shirt, jacket, and tie. The two-hour trip would give me enough time to plan the proposal.

Along the way, Katie shared a great deal about her family. Her dad was a corporate lawyer, and her mom was an architect. Suddenly, I was rattled. The idea of two parents or someone with a dad at home seemed foreign.

The further we traveled from my home, the more I realized we had less in common than I thought. Golf, art galleries, and gala dinners were a big part of her life. For me, basketball, moving from one apartment to another, and trying to keep clear of gangs were what I remember most of my childhood.

For me, the second-guessing continued when we tried to settle on a dial for the radio station. Hip Hop for me, and strangely enough, classical for her. I realized she was too far east, and I was too far west.

Later, she slept as I drove. I tried to drown out my doubts. I looked at her as she rested against the window, and I was wrong. From the start, we were meant to be. And everything was and is perfect.

We exited Interstate 91. Up ahead, the classic small town sign read "Mondhill, Population 7300, Home of True Southern Hospitality". We turned and entered a quiet suburban community. The GPS led us to the charming house Katie called home.

"Katie," I said in a whisper.

We made our way up the driveway. She rubbed the sleep from her eyes and perked up at the sight of home.

We parked behind an older white pickup truck that did not fit the picturesque scene. We stretched after exiting the car, but I couldn't help but stare in awe at the palatial estate. We made our way near the truck with the green stenciled letters on the door, which read "Ramon's Landscaping."

This forced me to admire the expanse of beautifully manicured grass as I followed Katie's steps along the cobblestone pathway leading to the front door.

Almost out of nowhere, a young, hulking man stepped in front of Katie and greeted her with a loving smile.

"Senorita Katie, I am so happy to see you," he said warmly.

Katie moved nearer to him before stepping back to introduce me.

"Oh, this is my…" she fumbled to find the right words, "Uh, a friend from school. Leroy."

My heart sank. A strapping young man appeared to have a great relationship with Katie, and I felt threatened by his good looks, muscular build, and a slight accent that made things sound romantic.

Ramon removed his gloves and firmly shook my hand. "Nice to meet you."

I barely smiled and replied, "Likewise."

Katie smiled again at him and then moved quickly towards the front door. And as she did, Ramon's eyes remained fixed on her.

"C'mon, Leroy," she said as she motioned towards the door.

"Chure a lucky man! Better take care of her," Ramon added in a near whisper.

I acted as though I didn't hear it and quickly found my rightful place next to Katie at the bottom of the steps leading to the house.

"What was that all about?" I blurted before realizing how demanding it must have sounded.

Puzzled by the question, Katie answered my question with her own, "What was what about?"

"Him."

"Ramon?"

"Yeah."

"Really? Jealous much?" she teased.

"I'm sorry. It's just, well, uh…" my words trailed off just as she started to explain.

"I love you, Leroy. Remember that. Ramon's dad worked for my family for years. Then, my father helped him bring his wife and son, Ramon, to America."

"Oh, so he's like hired help?"

"Oh no, he doesn't work here but feels forever indebted to my dad. Ramon owns a landscaping business and takes special care of our property. Anyways, he would do anything for my dad."

Satisfied with Katie's explanation, he smiled, playfully knocked on his head, and added, "Anyone home?"

Katie laughed, shook her head, and rolled her eyes before muttering, "Nice, the jealous type."

She opened the door, and they stepped into the foyer of the beautifully decorated home.

Sorry

Katie cupped her hands to her mouth, "Mom? Dad?" she hollered.

Her mom and dad quickly made their way down the grand staircase. They stopped short, balked, looked at their daughter, and then at me.

I held out my hand to greet Mr. Bradford. Her dad fumbled with his hands awkwardly before loosely shaking my hand.

"Leroy," I said, "nice to mee…" my words trailed off as Mr. Bradford interrupted.

"Have a seat in there," he ordered as he pointed to the den.

Puzzled, I proceeded to sit and questioned my presence there. Her dad and mom spoke to her in whispers, and they made their way quickly up the stairs.

From the room above, I could hear their voices growing louder. I felt uncomfortable.

I could only make out some of the words.

"But, Katie, you must understand."

"I love him."

"Katie, your grandma and… will… visiting. …can't allow…."

"But," Katie weakly protested.

Then silence.

"Yes, Mom. Okay, Dad," her voice cracking with emotion.

My heart sank. I stood to leave just as her dad entered the room. He was about to speak. The tears welling up in my eyes forced him to stop. I understood. I heard a muffled "I'm sorry" when I turned to the door.

I slowly meandered my way to the car hoping for Katie to run out to stop me. Just as I opened the door to the car, I looked at the windows above in hopes of catching a final glimpse. No luck. The words "I'm sorry" echoed in my ears.

I was in no condition to drive, but home would always be there. Waiting.

Sorry

My last thought was of holding her in my arms. Her beautiful skin. Her beautiful black skin

I didn't see the white truck.

TKO

One! ...Two!

The referee stood over him, yelling in a hoarse voice over the screams and shouts of the capacity crowd at Madison Square Garden.

...Three! ...Four!

Stop yelling, he thought. It stopped briefly as the referee's barrel chest heaved in a breath before continuing.

Where did he stop? Six?

Mom, Mom, please, one more story. Snuggled into bed with his oddly-colored stuffed animal, Marvin was comforted by the stories of kindness his mother weaved. With the story complete, he held tight to the lime-green elephant as he acted as though he were asleep and awaited a goodnight kiss. She moved closer and…

…Five! …Six!

If getting up stops his yelling, Marvin thought, I'll stand.

Reaching back, twenty-six-year-old Marvin Henry used the ropes to help himself up. Standing, yet his legs wobbled; more importantly, the yelling stopped. The referee tugged his wrists and forced him to hold out his arms.

"Continue," the white-haired referee bellowed.

His heart and mind were prepared to continue; however, the right side of his jaw yearned to return to the comforts of the blood-soaked mat.

With no desire to invite further punishment, Marvin tucked his elbows into his chiseled stomach muscles, crouched down low, and brought his black gloves in front of his face. Awaiting the sound of the bell to end the round, he held steadfast to this defensive posture. Blow after blow glanced off him. Time was not his friend. He waited.

The bell sounded. With his head bowed and eyes squinted tight, he tried drowning out everything. His Garden of Eden would be found on a small wooden stool in the blue corner.

Drifting. Henry felt as if he were above the ring watching his opponent, sporting red shorts and matching shoes, claiming victory for himself. His gloved arms raised high fueled the already raucous crowd and threw them into a frenzy. Barbaric, Henry thought.

Henry's longtime corner man, Sam-sam, quickly found his rightful place before the disfigured fighter. With only sixty seconds to perform a medical miracle, Sam-sam promptly assessed the damage and could only hope to repair Henry enough to survive another onslaught of leather. Sam-sam deftly applied ice to the areas of greatest need; the bridge of

Henry's bloodied nose, the welt just below the orbital bone of his left eye, and a fractured jaw. The cornerman shouted words of encouragement as he worked away. Unfortunately, his eyes betrayed the words as they revealed fear of an impending defeat. A sense of despair overcame Henry. Twenty-five seconds remained before the bell would signal the start of round six.

As usual, Henry's unorthodox coach remained outside the ring. Standing directly behind his star pupil, the coach remained quiet and reserved. He stood and looked over Henry's shoulder, and with a lifetime of experience as his guide, he analyzed the finer points of their current situation. And, to the dismay of the capacity crowd of twenty-two-odd thousand, the veteran coach stepped into the ring with the infamous white towel in hand. Fearing a premature end to this inevitable one-sided bloodbath, the fans began to boo and jeer in derision.

A spit bucket found its rightful place between Henry's boxing shoes. Like royalty,

Henry only had to tilt his jaw to the right, and a stream of refreshing water was delivered into his gaping mouth. As the water swished around, the balding coach stood before him, carrying over six decades of wisdom. Ashamed of his current state, Henry looked straight down at the spit bucket rather than look into the eyes of his coach.

Only a dozen seconds separated Henry's sabbatical from another round of one-sided brutality. The intensity and loudness of the booing reached a climax as the coach raised the towel next to Henry's right ear. The referee hastily made his way over to Henry's corner. Is he here genuinely to check on my health or ensure I am physically able to endure at least a few more punches? Henry thought. Satisfied with Sam-sam's quick work, the referee moved to the center of the ring in anticipation of the fighters meeting there again.

Wisely using the towel to shield his lips from the eyes of both fans and cameras, the coach spoke into Henry's ear.

The bell sounded. With unbelievable rage

and fury, Henry raced toward his opponent. Unleashing the inner beast within, Henry battered his opponent, not with jabs, but with a barrage of right hooks and uppercuts. The man ranked number two in the world did not stand a chance. Less than twenty seconds later, Desmond "The Dominator" Lawrence was no more. The referee didn't even bother to count. Unbeknownst to all in attendance, death found Lawrence even before his lifeless body crumpled to the mat.

Charleston Henry, Marvin's coach, stepped into the ring and embraced his son. Tears streamed down the embattled senior's tired face. Fourteen long years of sacrifice were bartered for this moment. Marvin Henry, one of the most feared fighters on the planet, was now the number-one challenger for the heavyweight crown.

Throngs of unrecognizable supporters filled the ring. And, with the announcer prepared to read the official result to signal the end of the fight, Charleston Henry reluctantly freed his son from an extraordinarily long embrace.

Marvin Henry stood next to the referee in anticipation of being announced as the winner by T.K.O. With the referee holding his arm high, Marvin looked around the wide girth of the ref in hopes of exchanging pleasantries with his previously undefeated opponent. However, in the celebration that followed the knockdown, Marvin had yet to notice Lawrence still lying motionless, surrounded by a team of doctors.

Amidst all the chaos, a spontaneous eruption of "Henry, Henry, Henry!" serenaded the young fighter by the turncoat crowd, many of whom were cheering on his impending defeat only moments earlier. Still reeling from the sight of his fallen rival, he had no interest in the celebrations reserved for his victory. Marvin Henry moved toward the neutral corner in a futile effort to escape everything. There, he silently prayed for Desmond Lawrence, his fallen rival.

Shocked by the destruction brought forth by his hands, raw emotions overcame him. His father noted the sudden change in his demeanor and quickly escorted him out of the ring and toward the dressing room. Henry would be fined at least five figures for exiting before the post-fight interview, but his Dad, now in the manager role, knew future endorsements were riding on his son saying all the right things. An emotionally-scarred pugilist was not what Charleston would present to the world.

A man now destined to fight for the world heavyweight title was back in the dressing room, sitting atop the trainer's table. It was a moment Henry had envisioned since he first donned the gloves, but now, for some strange reason, he felt the finish line had moved.

Post-fight protocol mandated immediate medical attention and a supervised urine sample. Unless Henry lacked a pulse, medical clearance was just a formality. The late-night would conclude with a post-fight press conference and an after-hours party at a private nightclub.

As a quiet man who often stuttered when nervous, the press conferences made Marvin most anxious. However, there was no escaping it. After his eighth fight as a pro, a single reporter from a local small-town paper covered the fight. However, with each victory, the cannibalistic media, which sought a piece of Marvin Henry, grew exponentially.

Tonight, the President's media relations team could not have prepared Henry for the group assembled. Flashes, lights, and a din of awe greeted his arrival. Henry was shown his spot at the all-too-familiar long table. However, the seats reserved for the defeated fighter and his coach remained vacant.

A barrage of questions was volleyed immediately. From the questions shouted, the one posed by a middle-aged man with a raspy voice drowned out the others. Now firmly established as the first questioner, the floor was now his.

"George Saki, New Hampshire Post. Congratulations, Marvin."

Marvin gave a respectful nod. "Thank you, S.S.., Su.., Suh."

"How would you assess tonight's performance?"

Since he was still experiencing a great deal of anxiety, Henry adopted a strategy recommended by his father. He tried his utmost to focus on the face of Alex Kerr, the reporter who first interviewed him.

Henry answered, "I..I, want to thththank Desmond. He fffought a perfect fffight. And I got lucky ththere at the end."

The standard post-fight questions were asked, and though, more often than not, responses by athletes are clichés, Marvin Henry was different. He would often pause, reflect, and process an answer fully before delivering it. Many believed it was his way of minimizing his speech impediment, but rather, it was something his mother had ingrained in him since he began to speak. What would God think about what I'm about to say? Marvin would ponder before answering. Thus, his responses were often brief yet always sincere.

Other than the size of the media gathered, there was nothing out of the ordinary. That is until a reporter from his hometown stood to deliver a pre-scripted question about his future fight plans. With her notepad ready, she started, "Kayla Palmer, Philadelphia Examiner. Mr. Henry, congratul.."

Another reporter, seated next to where Palmer stood, interrupted by whispering something in her direction. Ms. Palmer's eyes widened. She paused to regain her composure. Then, she closed her notepad. Staring blankly ahead, she started again. "Kayla Palmer, Philadelphia Examiner. Mr. Henry, How do you feel, uh… about the, um, announcement of Desmond Lawrence's death?"

The words punished Henry more than the blows he was fed earlier that evening. He leaned back until his ravaged body contoured to his chair. Then, Henry closed his eyes, bowed his head forward, and said another silent prayer.

Facing the cameras once again, tears welled up in his swollen eyes. "It, it, it's, uh…. I, I …." That was all he could muster. Whereas most fans and sports commentators opined that a boxer's death was an inherent risk that came with fighting for millions of dollars, Henry could only envision his opponent's seven-year-old son, Dee, sitting with his dad at the pre-fight weigh-in.

Marvin stood. Charleston rested his hand on his son's shoulder. Silence fell over the room. Everyone understood Marvin's desire to leave; unsurprisingly, there was a volley of questions from every reporter. After hastily collecting his belongings from his dressing room, he bade farewell to his exceptionally small entourage of four. Then he shared a few words with his father before exiting the always-welcoming New York night.

Everyone else meandered out of the room, leaving Marvin's father, Charleston Henry, alone amidst the photos of famed New York sports personalities from the Knicks and Rangers. He stared at the faces in the pictures.

If only, he thought. Team sports rarely present anything comparable to the tragedy he lived through tonight.

This victory and this night should have been a grand celebration. Marvin's supplanting Lawrence as the number one contender would inevitably immortalize both father and son in boxing history, and their lifelong dream would soon come to fruition. Instead, Charleston could only hope Marvin came to terms with this latest tragedy.

Charleston quickly grabbed his belongings and made his way toward one of the service exits. Six years of struggling to remain sober were soon to be drained away as he entered The Liberty, a bar on W. 35 Street. There, Charleston sought to drown his sorrows with a bottle of whiskey as his lone companion. Between the men's and women's washroom entrances near his table, the old jukebox played "Man of Constant Sorrow." The lyrics burrowed into his heart and forced him to reflect on the events of a complicated past.

After returning from Vietnam with a bullet

wound in his left leg, he had anticipated a hero's reception. Instead, months later, with a child on the way, Charleston's only welcome was to the back of the welfare line. And, like other soldiers before him, a social drinker was debased and transformed into a raging alcoholic.

Charleston's love of sports was his saving grace. When Marvin turned seven and began participating in sports, Charleston assumed a more active role as a parent. Sure, he still drank daily, but much of his leisure time was devoted to his son's hectic schedule.

Looking back, Charleston marveled at Marvin's athleticism. Even as an eight-year-old, he excelled and dominated older kids in all sports. However, the family's meager income limited Marvin's options to basketball, soccer, and boxing.

News stories about overbearing parents did nothing to dissuade Charleston from his desire to build, not develop, a sporting prodigy. Since boxing, unlike team sports, was based on individual performance, Charleston knew he would have total control over his son's development. No other players or coaches would influence young Marvin.

However, his wife, Leona, stood in the way of Charleston's grand plan. Her religious beliefs begot her pacifist views, and there was no way her son would ever wear boxing gloves. From the outset, Leona was adamant, yet Charleston figured she could be convinced before Marvin's twelfth birthday.

Once Marvin reached the age of ten, and only two years remained before his formal boxing training would begin, the marital conflicts became more frequent and intense. The hostilities between Leona and Charleston never waned and continued until she was murdered in a botched robbery of their desolate apartment. Detectives questioned Charleston on two occasions, but no one was ever charged.

Tears found a way to accompany Charleston and his whiskey at the back of the bar. He knew she'd be here with him if only Leona had just given them a chance.

As he sat there using his index finger to move the remnants of three ice cubes inside the empty glass, his thought turned to Marvin. He looked at his phone: no missed call and no message. "Dear God, take care of him," he whispered. Reaching into his wallet, he grabbed a crisp fifty-dollar bill. As was his habit, he crumpled it and placed it under the empty glass.

A faded photo of an emotionless twelve-year-old holding a boxing trophy was proudly displayed inside his Burberry wallet. Charleston vividly recalled the day the photo was taken. It was only six days after Marvin helped bury his mother. No one would ever question his son's resiliency, for it was something Charleston indoctrinated into him from the outset. In little time, Marvin mastered the skills and techniques of great boxers, yet Charleston was more concerned with the mental aspect of his lone student.

Sure, natural skill, technique, and strategy were critical to success in boxing, but Charleston viewed the sport not just as violence but as controlled violence. And the ability to focus would be at the core of Marvin's training. Far too often, Charleston thought, coaches expect athletes to persevere, but unless the coach trained them to persevere, it would be nothing but a ten-dollar word. Thus, Marvin's daily routine included performing mundane acts for two hours.

Charleston's teaching methods, albeit highly successful, bordered on mental abuse. The decisions he made as a coach would never yield to any concerns he may have had as a parent. Charleston sought opportunities to enrage young Marvin to fulfill his plan of creating a champion. Once his son had "snapped," Charleston would physically restrain him. Then, he would manipulate Marvin's emotions by redirecting his anger to the one tragedy Marvin could never escape - the horrific murder of his beloved mother.

The love Marvin and his mother shared transcended the deplorable conditions around them, and the love was irreplaceable. Only memories of that love remained. Fully aware of his son's emotional attachment to their nightly routine with the stuffed elephant, Charleston would use the elephant's name, Gweenzy, to provoke and trigger Marvin.

Fearful Marvin would inflict a bare-fisted assault on an unsuspecting bystander if someone inadvertently used a word similar to "Gweenzy," Charleston settled on "Gweenzy9" as the code word to unhinge Marvin.

With a perfect twenty-four TKOs in each of his two dozen professional fights, Charleston's strategy of using a phrase to unleash the maniacal monster within had worked perfectly. Success followed the pair up to and including tonight's big fight.

The unexpected vibration of his phone found a way to alert Charleston from his drunken stupor. His attempted grab at the phone almost sent the now-empty bottle crashing to the floor.

"Marvin?" groggily, his dad asked. He remained silent as Marvin explained how he stayed with Lawrence's family at the hospital, awaiting the release of his body.

"Yes, yes. I was drinking. O.K, I know, I know. I'll call tomorrow," he added before hanging up.

Like the pain of a loved one's death, news of Desmond Lawrence's death snaked from the front pages to the back and eventually faded to oblivion. But ten months later, articles relating to the death of Lawrence resurfaced with the announcement of Marvin Henry's championship fight in Berlin, Germany. He was scheduled to fight the undisputed Heavyweight Champion of the World, Borislav "The Beast" Bomba, a behemoth from Ukraine.

Initially, all questions and discussions focused on Marvin's role in the tragic death of Lawrence. As the fight date neared, and the world eagerly awaited the apparent mismatch, most pundits and social commentators' calls for eliminating boxing fell on deaf ears. In this case, the `David versus Goliath' hyperbole employed by the promoter may have been closer to fact than fiction. At the weigh-in, Marvin's 6'3" frame supported an even 250 pounds, whereas Bomba measured 6'11" and tipped the scale at 303.

For the championship fight, Charleston modified Marvin's training program, and all he required was a single opportunity to use the code word. The coach aimed to have Marvin build his overall power yet maintain the advantages of speed and agility he held over Bomba. And more importantly, if Marvin remained standing as the fight entered round four, the larger Bomba would have expended most of his energy, and "Gweenzy9" would be the final stepping stone to success.

Two weeks before the fight, they had arrived in Germany to much fanfare. And although Las Vegas had Marvin Henry as a four-to-one underdog on the day of the fight, Charleston remained confident he would coach Marvin to the heavyweight title.

Only hours before the fight, Charleston fell ill. Unable to join Marvin at the biggest fight of his career, Charleston would be forced to watch the proceedings live via pay-per-view from his hotel room. Charleston was unconcerned with his failing health, but rather how he would convey the words "Gweenzy9" to Marvin.

Trusting someone to deliver the words was not the issue. Instead, Charleston had to ensure the phrase was never shared or spoken again. After much thought, he decided Sam-sam, his loyal friend of over thirty years, would be his only option.

"Sam-sam?" Charleston tried to call over the ESPN analysts' pre-fight predictions being broadcasted in his room.

Sam-sam, who was admiring the view of the Fernsehturn as it stood along the Berlin skyline, hurried over. "Everything O.K, Boss?"

"Yeah, yeah. I should be there tonight."

"No, you need to rest for the celebration tonight."

Charleston smiled at the thought. "Look, I need you to do something important. In every fight wherein Marvin faced a real challenge, I would wait until his opponent had started to show signs of fatigue. Once the bell sounded to end the round, I would let you do your thing. But just before the ref signaled the start of the next round, I would say a phrase into Marvin's ear. And that's what brought out the animal in him."

"Ya kidding me, right?"

"Of course not; everyone thinks Marvin begins to attack at the perfect opportunity. Well, he does, but the phrase triggers the rage, you see."

Standing dumbfounded, Sam-sam could only shake his head in disbelief. "I can't believe that I missed it. You mean YOU would be the one that lit the fire under Marvin's ass?"

"Damn straight."

"Unreal, unfreaking real!"

"And since I can't be there, I need someone to do it. Sam-sam, you have been with us from the start, and you know how much the boy has been through with his mom and my past...." The words hung there for a brief moment.

"Of course, Boss. You have been a loyal friend. Of course, I'll do it."

"I need you to remember a few things,

however. One, wait til Bomba looks tired. Two, say the word clearly into his right ear just before the referee signals the start of the round. Cover your mouth with the towel so no one can make out your words. And, I need you to never utter the word again to anyone, not even as a joke."

"I promise, Boss. You know I have you covered."

"Thanks. But, repeat the steps back to me."

"One, Bomba has to be tired. Two, say the word into Marv's right ear. Three..."

"No, make sure you say it when the ref is about to start the round. Sam-sam, the timing is critical."

"Got it. One, Bomba was tired. Two, the word in the right ear at the ref's signal. Three, use the towel as a shield. Four, erase the word from my memory."

"Sam-sam, this is it. Marvin will be the World Heavyweight Champion if you can do this!"

The thought brought a genuine smile to

Sam-sam's face. Sam-sam, the trainer for the Heavyweight Champion of the World, he said to himself.

Sam-sam knew too much. Charleston concluded that Sam-sam's love of gambling and the possible misuse of the code word meant eliminating him would be a priority after the fight. But for now, Sam-sam was needed.

Bomba came out seeking to annihilate Marvin in the early rounds that night. Marvin ducked, weaved, and was able to slip in a few solid jabs. But, in the fourth round, a crushing right hook that caught Marvin above the left ear knocked him down. Down for the count, the referee reached eight on a slow count before Marvin could get his legs firmly under him. With only seven seconds remaining in the fourth round, Marvin was able to withstand the late flurry of solid shots from Bomba.

In bed, Charleston's blood pressure climbed as he watched his son take punch after punch. His limbs ached, and soreness around his war wound intensified. This had only happened to him once, twenty years ago. The paralysis of his body had started from his injured leg, and unless he took medication, death would ensnare him. His body shook violently, and with no help or phone in sight, he could only stare at the TV screen.

Before the start of the fifth round, Sam-sam knew he had to act. He did precisely as Charleston had said, and thirty-two seconds later, the mat shook as Bomba's 300-plus pound body fell with a thud. The crowd erupted with cheers as the new champion, Marvin Henry, stood at the center of the ring with great humility.

Incredible wealth and fame would now find the Henrys. Marvin couldn't wait to embrace his Dad. He was gracious and complimented Bomba in his post-fight interview and press conference. And, with tears streaming down his battered face, he thanked his mentor, coach, hero, and dad, Charleston. Of course, as always, he pointed to the sky and remembered his beloved Mom and even Desmond Lawrence. And in a genuinely touching moment that captured the world's attention, Marvin dedicated the win to Desmond's son, Dee.

Much like the end of the previous fight, Marvin's thoughts were elsewhere. The after-hours celebration would have to wait. Marvin quickly gathered his belongings, including his new hardware, the world heavyweight championship belt. He was taken via limousine to the swanky Casa Camper Berlin to savor the victory with his Dad.

Marvin found his Dad propped up on two pillows with the TV replaying highlights of the big fight. Charleston smiled as Marvin raced in with the championship belt draped over his shoulder.

"Dad, Dad, we did it! We did it!" Marvin exclaimed.

Charleston nodded his head at the TV and smiled again. "Sorry, the volume is a 'lil loud."

Marvin grabbed the remote and hit the mute button. Fearing the end may be near, he ran his hand over his father's head. "I love you, Dad. Ttthank you."

"I'll be okay, son," Charleston said with conviction. "This same thing happened about twenty years ago, and the specialist in Philadelphia prescribed a drug that worked. But I don't recall his name or the drug's name."

"Wwhere's it hhurt?"

"All over, but I need the meds for this. And.." A series of violent coughs interrupted him. "I know, wait. The name of the drug may be found in my Gmail account."

Marvin quickly took to his phone. "W..w..what account, Dad?"

"Go to Gmail. It's all lowercase: marvinchamp at gmail dot com."

The son furiously typed away on his phone's keypad.

"Oh my God, Dad!" Marvin realized he had yet to call for assistance. "Let me call for help."

Marvin grabbed the phone from the other room and called 9-1-1.

Racing back into the room, he found his

Dad still alert.

"O.KK.. Dad, what's the password?"

"It's g-w-e-e-n-z-y with the number nine."

"Gweenzy? Like my elephant?"

"Yes, son."

"Gweenzynine?"

When the emergency personnel arrived, Charleston Henry had died. His face was bloodied, battered, and unrecognizable beyond belief.

Marvin Henry, the new world heavyweight champion, was led away in handcuffs.

THE TICKET

She held the crumpled slip of paper inside her clenched fist. Holding a five-dollar bill in the other hand, the scraggly-dressed Ms. Lucas pleaded with the shopkeeper to buy another lottery ticket.

"Rules are rules, Ms. Lucas," the proprietor of Barry's General Store explained, "the government made it clear; only one ticket can be registered to each family."

"Please, Mr. Barry, I'll give you double."

With no other customers within earshot, Mr. Barry thought, why not. He took Ms. Lucas' five dollars and waited as she reached into her purse for another.

Mr. Barry took the other bill, looked around, and added, "Can never be too safe." He entered her surname and the last three digits of her Social Security Number into the computer terminal for the second time in as many minutes. Awaiting a second chance at a life of freedom, Ms. Lucas craned her neck to read the operator's screen. The terminal beeped twice and returned only a small slip that read in caps, "TRANSACTION DECLINED."

"Whaaat?" Mr. Barry grunted as he slapped his hand on the counter.

Ms. Lucas held out her hand.

"As I told you, Ms. Lucas," he said as he returned her money, "the government organized this lottery unlike any other. The new president is a little radical in his approach, but somehow he's still practical, ya know."

"Well, thanks for trying."

"Yeah, I'm glad he'll stop all those immigrants and their cheating ways," he boldly added, further demonstrating his unwavering support.

Tempted to respond, Ms. Lucas instead held her tongue and made a beeline exit. A fifty-dollar bill lay on the porch of the historically-preserved building, just at the edge of the wooden steps. Having never had anything greater than a twenty, Ms. Lucas nearly sidestepped it. She placed her bag down, casually looked to see if any wandering eyes noticed, and then subtly retrieved it. She waited. Still, no one claimed it.

Leaving her bag unattended, Ms. Lucas marched back into the store. Explaining how she found the bill, she handed it to Mr. Barry, hoping it would be returned to its rightful owner. Shocked at the strong moral compass of this apparent societal outcast, he took the bill and stood with his mouth agape as she turned away and headed towards the door.

Only five hours remained until the big draw. But being entitled to only one ticket did little to stir any hope.

It's unfair for the nearest store registered to sell to be way out here, she thought. Not being able to purchase more than one ticket would make the journey back home feel longer. Carrying her plastic grocery bag in one hand, the urge to examine the ticket forced her to make an early stop.

As she approached a bus stop bench, the person in the center moved to the extreme right. Instinctively, Ms. Lucas placed her bag in the middle and found her place on the left. Ms. Lucas uncurled her fingers and straightened the ticket on her leg. Slowly and discreetly, the man on the bench glanced at the ticket.

Trying to find the right words to initiate a conversation, he asked, "Ah, got your ticket, huh?"

Ms. Lucas preferred to be left to her thoughts, but the popularity of this lottery made it the topic of discussion nationwide. She relented.

"Yeah, had to leave the farm work and walk across the state line just to get it," she complained.

"I don't buy lottery tickets," he responded with a sense of superiority but added, "What does it say?"

With the back of the ticket already facing her and feeling obligated to share, Ms. Lucas read, "First Pr.. Pre.. Presi.. Presidential National Lottery to be held on August 8 at 3:00 P.M. at the Pr..Presidential Palace. Five numbers will be drawn for a grand prize of eighty million dollars."

Still fully interested in a lottery he had no chance of winning, the young man asked, "How many numbers ya need to win?"

Puzzled by questions to which everyone knew the answers, she blurted, "Have ya been livin' under a rock?"

"Well, Madame, I just returned today from service overseas. Being away for two years, you kinda learn to focus on more important things like survival," he responded with a twinge of resentment.

"Oh, didn't mean no harm. Just surprised since that's all folks been talkin' about since the announcement."

"I understand," he said sincerely and then added, "So how's it all work?"

Turning the ticket over, she examined it and noted, "Well, there are only five digits." She mentally noted the randomly generated numbers 3, 7, 11, 33, and 77 and saw them as a good omen. Her little angel Ellie's birthday is November 3, and 7 has always been her favorite number. She flipped the ticket over again and added, "Says here, the available numbers are one to eighty-eight."

Surprised at the near-impossible odds, he tried to clarify, "You mean there'll be eighty-eight balls, and five will be drawn for the grand prize of eighty million?"

"That's what it says here," she answered as she pointed to the ticket.

'Wow, eighty million big ones. It'll sure help a family change their fortunes."

"The new president," she said with a hint of bitterness, "sure has an odd way of doing things."

"Glad I voted for President Stong," the young soldier proudly affirmed.

With a trace of guilt, Ms. Lucas nodded in agreement while hiding that she didn't care for the President's divisive views.

Just as the two strangers began to feel comfortable with each other, the roar of a diesel-engine bus could be heard as it advanced toward them.

"Ah, here's the bus," he noted unnecessarily.

"Oh, I just sat here to rest."

He picked up his overstuffed khaki backpack from beside the bench and stood. He reached into the pocket of his issued uniform pants for a bus ticket and tried to end his part of the conversation with a question, "Oh, you live near here?"

"Nah, not a city folk; I'm from around

Lula," she proudly claimed.

He stared in disbelief and exclaimed, "Mississippi? That's a four-and-a-half-hour walk!"

Reminded about the inevitable long walk which awaited, she stood. Ms. Lucas took hold of the grocery bag and just nodded at him. He boarded the bus and watched her through one of the large dirt-covered windows.

Purchasing a lottery ticket, followed by a thirteen-mile walk along the back roads, would give her ample time to dream of life after the big win. But things have never come easy for Susan Lucas. The second of seven children, she was only fourteen when her mother was diagnosed with leukemia. Thus, the role of caregiver was thrust upon her. And less than three months later, the finality of her mom's death forced even more responsibilities upon her slender shoulders.

Walking swiftly during the first mile of thirteen, Ms. Lucas looked across the dirt road and marveled at the simple design of a small one-room schoolhouse. Blanketed in white paint, only a large bell atop the entrance and "Ol' Glory" frayed at the edges distinguished it from the local churches. The mere sight of a school forced Ms. Lucas to recollect the best memories of her childhood.

As far back as anyone could remember, Susan enjoyed playing a game oddly named "Teacher, teacher." With dolls and small barnyard animals as her students, Susan would dress in her "Sunday Best" and lead simple counting and alphabet lessons to her inattentive and unsuspecting "students."

Years later, Susan would cajole her younger brothers and sisters to form a straight line, enter the barn, which always served as her classroom, and proceed to preach about the Lord.

Ms. Lucas. It had a nice ring to it, she thought. Encouraging her younger siblings to call her by this respectful title during "Teacher, teacher" games further added to its familiarity.

For young girls, the thought of being a teacher is not uncommon. However, the vividness of Susan's imagination was unparalleled. In her mind, it would always be near summer's end as the crisp coolness welcomed an early September morning. She imagined walking into a Kindergarten class on the first day of school with exactly twenty-six girls.

Making the experience even more special was that each student's name would begin with a different letter of the alphabet. Sometimes, as she dramatized it, Susan would melodiously read out the names from an attendance roster in a voice only she could hear. And she would always respond as well.

Anna. Present.

Beatrice, Present.

Carol. Present.

Daphne. Silence. Daphne. Oh, present.

Ellie.

And this would continue until she concluded with Zoe.

But, unfortunately for Susan Lucas, her imagination surpassed reality. Not only did her mother's demise add to an already heavy burden of school and farm work, but it crushed Susan's dreams of teaching kindergarten. And her vivid imagination, like her dreams, was crushed by the final closing of her mother's eyes.

The distinctive sounds of the steel rails from afar returned Susan's thoughts to her immediate surroundings.

As Ms. Lucas journeyed along the desolate road, she occasionally looked across the open fields toward the horizon. A lone figure towering over a vacant field caught her eye. She stopped. Raising her hand to shade her eyes from the sun's glare, the haunting face of a disproportionately built scarecrow stared back at her. Fear overtook her as a flash of memories burrowed into her thoughts.

Standing still at the side of the road, Ms. Lucas' mind recollected a traumatic event from when she was just sixteen. She recalled being in the field collecting the early harvest. Standing at the base of a scarecrow she helped fashion with her sisters, she heard the rustling of bushes nearby. She assumed it to be Benji, her oft-teasing nine-year-old brother. Instead, there stood Mr. Daley.

Being at the mercy of a landowner was never easy for the Lucas family. However, renting from the merciless Mr. Daley was unbearable. Even more so for Susan as she was forced to sacrifice more and more to the old man's whims and desires.

Young Susan often heard everyone remembers their first time. All she ever recalled of the horrifying ordeal was the sight of a smiling scarecrow looking down at her as she fumbled to cover her blood-stained body.

Months later, as her body began to show signs of pregnancy, Susan was shamed into leaving home. Even after a miscarriage, eleven agonizingly long and unjustly shameful months passed before she would return home.

Once again, Susan tried her utmost to keep the family together. However, cheap local whiskey abetted Dad with an escape, and the four youngest Lucas children became wards of the state.

The loud and repetitive caws of a crow flying nearby startled Susan from her trance. She almost mechanically continued her trek without considering time or destination, so she just walked.

Again, recalling her dreams of teaching kindergarten, Ms. Lucas would envision each child's hair, face, smile, and clothes. Anna. Ms. Lucas thought of her often. She smiled at the thought of Anna's long auburn hair lapping over those beady, chestnut-brown eyes. Those eyes often masked her beguiling ways. Her little Anna, Susan loved her as she loved all the others.

The breeze from across the vast expanse of fields reawakened her senses. And, only two miles from where the scarecrow reopened old wounds from her difficult past, Ms. Lucas approached Gemstone Baptist Church ahead on her right. Memories of her wedding day overtook her thoughts. The words "for better or for worse" rang in her ears. Susan's hopes for a better life away from the hard work of the farm were realized when Minister Edwards uttered the words, "I now pronounce you man and wife" to Susan and Carson Williams.

Carlson Williams had been a successful investment banker specializing in securing farmers' loans. With tales of the bright lights and big city, William's pitch to invest convinced even the most cynical in town. His allure also captivated Susan's heart.

Unbeknownst to all, Williams used his conniving ways on eleven unsuspecting families. With their signatures on various documents, Williams granted himself power of attorney to sell their fall harvest. The 700 acres toiled over from spring to fall by the eleven families netted Williams over a quarter of a million dollars. For the investors, there was nothing. Worse still, all were left homeless.

The Ticket

Susan's hands, hardened by years of hard work, were matched only by years of regret and remorse that had forged her heart. Emotionally shattered far too many times in one lifetime, Susan Lucas was forced to seek the silver lining.

Not bothered by the start of light rain, Ms. Lucas continued along the abandoned dirt road while her horrid past continued to torment her.

About halfway home, she crossed the rickety bridge spanning the Mississippi River. Tired and beaten by life, Ms. Lucas continued along the neglected Highway 49.

On "49", she paused and stared wonderfully at the abandoned red barns lining each side of the dirt road to form a symmetrical image. A painter's dream, she thought.

A subtle smile appeared on her weary face. Looking at the symmetry again, the twins Beatrice and Carol came to mind. Always dressed in matching outfits, their short blonde hair curtained their round faces, further accentuating their bottle-green eyes. While

Beatrice remained reserved, her twin Carol would share the most insignificant details of the most trivial events. But Ms. Lucas would listen, for the twins were hers to love.

Finally, after four hours of walking, familiar sights at the edge of her hometown became more frequent as she crossed that imaginary boundary between home and away.

The rain intensified as she approached the lifeless intersection of Highway 49 and the grass-covered, rusted rail tracks referred to as "The Crossroads."

Ms. Lucas found an old, beaten wooden bench, the last relic of a defunct railroad stop over twenty years ago. As the skies darkened with the approach of a summer storm, Ms. Lucas planned to sit for a few moments before undertaking the final leg of her journey. Exposed to and abused by the elements, the naked bench hardly served its simple purpose.

The heavy rains began to assault and soak through her porous jacket. Just as Ms. Lucas rested her grocery bag on the bench, she noticed some words carved into the decrepit wood. Taking the calloused tip of her index finger, she traced over the letters to make out their meaning. Robert Johnson was here, she said to herself.

A short man in a trench coat stealthily approached her from just south of "The Crossroads." Ms. Lucas caught a glimpse of him, but with little concern for her well-being, she sat with her two devoted companions: regret and remorse.

The man appeared before her and looked into the face of a woman who had lived many lives. Nodding from under a fedora, his face offered only a blank stare.

Then, Ms. Lucas noticed he showed no signs of rain. Puzzled, she glanced around where he stood and found the dirt roads muddied. She was dumbfounded, but her past prepared her for a cruel end.

The man held his left hand out before her. Gloved and balled into a tight fist with the palm facing down, he slowly turned it over and extended his thumb, followed by each finger one by one. In his hand lay a crisp lottery ticket, and he extended it to her. But before he handed it over, he cupped his hands around his mouth, moved his face next to her cheek, and whispered words that would never be repeated.

Looking directly into his eyes, she nodded in agreement and took ownership of the ticket. She glanced at the five numbers: 4, 6, 13, 27, and 66. Unlucky and evil, she thought.

The ominous 13 stood out first, and the 27th of July was her wedding date. And finally, 6 and 66.

The man's left hand closed, and then it reopened. With his gloved fingers pointing towards her and the palm still facing upwards, he awaited something in return.

"Your other ticket, Ms. Lucas," he demanded.

"B...b...but it's registered to me," she meekly protested.

Answering first with an icy stare, he stated

in a deep monotone voice, "Both tickets share the same registration code."

Already in possession of the new ticket he had offered, Ms. Lucas felt obligated to complete the transaction. Confused, she reached into her pocket and pulled out the wet slip of paper. For the final time, she looked at the favorable numbers on the ticket purchased just hours earlier. She yielded it to him with a sigh as her only form of protest.

Ms. Lucas placed the new ticket into the wet pocket of her beaten jacket. Then, placing her hand on the grocery bag handles, she was fully prepared to leave. The man was nowhere in sight. She looked into the distance of "The Crossroads." Resigned to fate, home, she thought.

Still reeling from the strange meeting, Ms. Lucas tried to distract herself by recalling the attendance list of names in a singsong fashion. An-na, Bea-trice, Car-ol, and… she felt horrible. How is it possible to forget, she thought. With greater focus, she started again: Anna, Beatrice, Carol, Daphne… Yes, Daphne, she said aloud.

Again, the memories of the children made her feel loved. A smile reappeared. Daphne. A real firecracker, she recalled. Daphne was the most rebellious, with her strawberry-blonde mop of curls complementing her pale skin. Ms. Lucas recalled little else about her. Like all classes, students came and went; some spent much less time with Ms. Lucas than others. She still held a warm spot for the smiling five-year-old Daphne, whom she teasingly called "Daffy."

The sound of thunder in the distance made Ms. Lucas conscious of her immediate surroundings. She pulled at the collars of her jacket in a feeble attempt to shield herself from the rain. The long walk continued.

Despite the "unlucky" numbers, hope slowly renewed as she neared home. Now, just like everyone else, she thought someone must win. "Why not me?" she said in a whisper. "Why not me?" she repeated. Imagining the possibilities if she won, she picked up the pace.

Ms. Lucas planned to share the winnings with her two remaining siblings. And at home, eleven-year-old Ellie could once again experience a real birthday party with a cake and presents.

Feeling parched, Ms. Lucas stopped at the local store to buy a soda. Grabbing a bottle of root beer from the noisy refrigerator at the back of the store, she headed straight to the counter in hopes of arriving home soon. In front of her was a girl no older than nine having difficulty counting a handful of pennies and nickels while balancing an ice cream.

Despite feeling thirsty, hungry, and tired, Ms. Lucas held steadfast to the idea of winning the lottery. Surprisingly, even to herself, Ms. Lucas took out a dollar bill, stepped in front of the girl, and offered to pay for her ice cream.

Mr. Hazell, the long-time storekeeper, stared in disbelief and asked, "Are you sure, Ms. Lucas?"

"Sure, why not?"

Smiling, he joked, "Oh, okay, no problem here, so long as it's cash." He laughed at his little joke as Ms. Lucas looked on in silence.

Ms. Lucas politely smiled, collected the pennies and nickels scattered about the counter, and returned them to the young girl. The girl smiled and stuffed the coins in her faded blue jeans pocket before enjoying the vanilla ice cream.

She looked at Ms. Lucas and said, "Thank you, Ma'am."

"You're welcome, dear."

"I'm Fiona, and I'll be eight on Sunday."

Enchanted by the name she heard, Ms. Lucas sought to clarify, "Did you say Fiona?"

"Yes."

"Well, I'm so pleased to meet you, and Happy Birthday!"

She hastily left the store and quickened her pace to make up for some lost time.

Arriving in her hometown almost five

hours after buying the lottery ticket, thoughts of spending money began to feel like a betrayal of her modest upbringing.

Ms. Lucas' childhood was bound to Rich, Mississippi, a quiet farm town. With little money, as a child, shopping with her parents was like experiencing colorless dreams wherein desires always exceeded reality.

She'd often noticed other children with toys at the checkout, some throwing tantrums, and even a few carrying wish lists. For her, stores only served as a reminder of her family's plight. Too far down to dream of things so high, she thought. Detaching herself and remaining emotionless was her saving grace.

As she reached the porch of her home, Ms. Lucas reached into her pocket and felt the ticket; her lease to a new life.

Oddly enough, though Ms. Lucas' home was bereft of hope, it was always filled with love. Home was a welcomed sight.

"Oh, Mom, how I missed you," Ellie greeted her.

"I'm so sorry. The walk took longer than expected."

"Here, let me help you."

Ms. Lucas smiled as Ellie took her coat and the groceries.

Ellie. After the annulment of her marriage, years of loneliness followed. A growing void in her heart was left unfulfilled. She was alone after years together with a large family on the farm. She realized isolation is the most damning thing to the human spirit. Then things changed. And now, the one redeeming aspect of her cruel life was Ellie. She paused and contemplated for a moment. She mused that Fiona, the little girl at the store, reminded her of a younger Ellie.

"Come, Mom, I made you soup with the vegetables from the yard."

"Oh my, I could use a warm bowl of soup, my dear."

Together, they sat at the square table that had been painted too often. Their home, a single room with a small kitchen and bathroom, desperately needed attention. Dimly lit, the odd-shaped homemade candle set on the table provided a dull orange glow in the sparsely furnished room.

"Did you get a ticket, Mom?"

"Yes, dear. We'll listen to the broadcast together."

Unconvinced of any hope, Ellie shared a forced smile

"Ellie, dear, I'll have the soup later. Please turn on the radio."

Ms. Lucas felt pleased as the young girl immediately moved towards the radio and tuned it for clarity.

"Thank you, dear," Ms. Lucas politely added.

Ms. Lucas reached behind where she sat and took hold of her jacket from the sofa near the entrance. She placed the coat on her lap and fished inside her pocket for the ticket. Looking at the numbers, a sense of resignation overcame her. Hopelessness.

Ellie noticed the time and turned the volume up on the radio. Ms. Lucas placed the ticket on the table. Suddenly, they felt obligated to assume the roles of hopeful participants. But both knew better.

Ellie looked closely at the ticket. "13, 6, and 66?" Ellie questioned just above a whisper.

"It's okay, dear, the shopkeeper just handed us our lot," Ms. Lucas lied as she avoided mention of her meeting at The Crossroads.

"It's about to start," Ellie noted as great excitement filled the banal existence of a nation.

They remained seated at the table with only the ticket and a lit candle between them. The sound from the radio echoed throughout the tiny home.

HOST: "Good Afternoon, and welcome to the live broadcast of one of the most captivating moments in our nation's history. I am William Feldberg, and right here at the Presidential

Palace in Washington D.C., the winning numbers for the First National Presidential Lottery will be drawn. Mr. President, a few words, please."

Applause

PRESIDENT STONG: "Welcome to the First National Presidential Lottery. As the 46th President, I pledged to make great changes and restore our nation to its glory. For many years, those who do not share our way of life have extinguished our dreams. Those who come like scavengers reaping from our efforts erode our hard work. I promised change, and today I stand here before the nation with change. The First National Presidential Lottery is another step towards making our nation great."

HOST: "There you have it. And now, the moment you all have been waiting for. Under the supervision of the Porter, Young, and Miyata Auditing Firm in Manhattan, New York, our lovely model will place the balls numbered 1 through 88 into the drum."

"President Stong, if you may honor us by

pushing the button to start the spinning of the drum."

"Ten seconds on the counter, please."

"Now, Mr. President, if you can again press the button to stop the machine and release the five balls."

"The numbers have been drawn; we will reveal one at a time."

"The first number is 27. I repeat, 27.

"The second number, 13. Again, the second number is 13.

"The third number, 4. So we have 27, 13, and now 4."

Ellie and Ms. Lucas focused on the ticket until the third number was announced. They both started to look up but then stopped, fearing it might jinx their unprecedented good fortune.

HOST: "The fourth number is 6. I repeat 6."

Ms. Lucas extended her hands across the table, and Ellie placed her hands into hers. Ms.

Lucas held tight. A sense of hope was aroused in both.

The host sought to build excitement by delaying the announcement of the final number. Ms. Lucas and Ellie gave in and finally looked at one another.

HOST: "The fifth and final number is… 66. So, to repeat, the winning numbers in numerical order are 4, 6, 13, 27, and 66."

Ms. Lucas couldn't believe it. Her difficult life finally kicked away at the darkness to bleed a glorious light. Remorse and regret had now been replaced by hope and happiness. She held tight to Ellie's hands, and the tears began to flow.

Making out each syllable, Ms. Lucas slowly repeated the winning amount, "Eighty million dollars...eighty million dollars."

They would now enjoy a life of luxury. Then, Ms. Lucas looked at Ellie. The media would soon descend upon them and their meager existence. Worse still, everything would change once the media exposed Ms. Lucas' sordid past to the entire nation.

Susan Lucas focused her eyes on the ticket. Glancing around her home, resignation gripped her. A sense of hopelessness again enveloped her, and her past would continue to haunt her.

Ellie looked at her Mom's face as it contorted into an unfamiliar look of bewilderment. Recalling the final words whispered by the short man at "The Crossroads," Ms. Lucas knew she had to act quickly and do the inconceivable. The ticket was the only window into her past.

"Ellie, dear, could you please get me a glass of water?"

Obediently, without even answering, Ellie proceeded to the tap.

With Ellie's back to her, Ms. Lucas picked up the ticket. The swaying flame of the candle invited her to be free of the burden. Her hand trembled as she edged the ticket closer to the flame. The ticket started to darken at the corner. Ms. Lucas sighed. The sound of the tap closing startled her. Instinctively, she pulled the ticket away and squeezed the slightly charred corner between her thumb and forefinger.

Oblivious to her Mom's actions, Ellie returned to the table. Ellie's right hand grasped the side of the glass while her left hand guided it from beneath. She handed the glass of water to her Mom with the utmost respect and grace.

A genuine smile appeared on Ms. Lucas' face. A life of luxury did await. Like Mr. Daley, the secrets of the past would remain concealed forever. The throngs of expected media would only share Ms. Lucas' rags-to-riches story, and never would they utter the names of those lives who intersected with Ms. Lucas—even Ellie's.

For in a nearby field, already littered with the bodies of Anna, Beatrice, Carol, and Daphne, the other children she had abducted, Ms. Lucas dumped Ellie's lifeless body.

And somewhere, Fiona again shared the story of a stranger who surprised her with an unexpected gift.

AUTHOR BIO

Mohamed Haniff Nana was born in Hamilton, Ontario, Canada. His parents, originally from India, immigrated to Canada from Barbados in 1967. He attended York University in Toronto, completing his Honors Degree in History with a minor in Geography. He has also completed his Bachelor of Education Degree and Principals' Qualification Courses.

Since elementary school, his curiosity and many exemplary teachers inspired him to write. Still, after graduation, busy with university, work, and family life, he had left all his writing to collect dust. During that time, he taught elementary school students for over twenty-five years. After sharing the writing process with his grade four, he was inspired to write and share his stories once again.

As a Muslim, he sports a long beard and traditional Islamic attire. At the same time, as a proud Canadian, one may also find him wearing a Hamilton Tiger-Cats jersey, baseball cap, and jeans. He is the proud parent of four children. Oh, and he has a very affectionate cat named Mocha.

MZP   Azhar I.   AMM
Bakharia & Hafejee Families

O.M. MacKillop P.S. - '75-'84

Ms.Bowles   Ms.Clark   Mr.Demisch   Mr.Hazell   Ms.Hoffer
Mr.Hunt   Ms.Klein   Ms.Lawrence   Ms.Rogers
Mr.Smith   Ms.Spencer   Mr.Tadros

Bayview S.S - '84-'90

Ms. Bracken   Mr.Fehlberg   Mr.Lawrence
Ms.Liasi   Mr.McKillop   Mr.Smith   Ms.Thompson

Laverock

David (Wasim) Ali   Derrick Atkinson   Merrick Atkinson
Sylvia Barron   Billy Corless   Steve Dizes   Gus Douboulidis
Stella Douboulidis   Jennifer Georgiev   Joanne Georgiev
Imtiaz (MT) Hosein   Everett Leaven   Steven Leaven
Andrew Orfanakos   Sam Orfanakos   Kathy Orfanakos
Colin Phillips   Curt Phillips   "Zak" Patel   Zuber Patel
Jimmy Polyvos   Mina Polyvos   Jeff Wright

O.M. MacKillop

Susan Armstrong   Clive Atkinson   Sharon Barron   Sandy Beck
Paul Black   Croy Bott   Mike Brown   Bob Cairns   Scott Campbell
Carlo Cotrone   Heather Cox   Kevin Crosby   Kristi DeBacker
Dorothy Fontaine   Erin Foot   Liz Grigordiadis   Roland Heider
Kristy Hook   Joyce Kline   Nancy McFee   Lori Newstead   Safia Patel
Michelle Pennock   Derek Plaxton   Tracy Robinson   Jim Ross
Chris Timperon   Erika Van Stratton   Lisa Vettese   Meg Williams
Angela Zeppeiri

Trishan Arul   Ryan Gamna   Anthony Gumbs   Shahe Kassardjian
Chris Kernohan   Pedro Mendes   AbdulMuqsit-Mick McDonald
Derek Pinto   Craig Rowland   Sandy Song   Jeff Stewart

Amesbury MS   Cedarwood PS
Crosby Heights PS   Pauline Johnson Jr PS